Beinn Dubh

Bog

Castle Rannoch

Upper Glen

Pond

R. Shael

Lower Glen

Mad Margaret's
Rock

D1094396

Sketch Map of
*GLENSHAEL*
& District.

South
ish,
ohn.

# Highland Masquerade

# Highland Masquerade

by Mary Elgin

## M. S. Mill Co.

*distributed by*
*William Morrow & Co., Inc.*
*New York, 1966*

Published in Great Britain
under the title *Return to Glenshael*

To
Walter
With My Love

The characters in this book are all imaginary and therefore no reference to anyone living or dead is possible.

The places are invented and exist only on the map provided.

But the chapter headings will be found in the Scottish Country Dance Books and the dances can be watched at nearly any Highland Ball.

# Contents

Highland
Masquerade

# 1

## Foursome Reel

Scene One: a railway carriage. Enter four characters to occupy the cornerseats. Two men, two women, masked as strangers are. Wise after the event—how odd this seems.

Backcloth, a Glasgow station, little changed. Ten years since I last saw it through younger, desperate eyes. I should feel sentimental, or at least excited, for I was going home to Glenshael.

I could not know that the curtain was to rise on a mad dance. The tune was called, slow-time at first, and we began to reel, passing and repassing; we improvised, clapped for the change of rhythm, to set and swing until we reached the final bow.

The sudden longing, quite unbearable in London, had now receded. As usual I'd been too impulsive. I was searching for another job when the name Glenshael leapt out of the close print of my newspaper. To think that a writer should live there and need a secretary—at Holly

Bank, of all places! It was a sort of miracle. For surely it was meant, and meant for me. I had not known how much I wanted home.

Once, a long time ago, there'd been a girl called Aillie Rannoch. . . .

An agent, only too eager to fix the matter up, interviewed me. James Bywater, my new employer, preferred dreary applicants; my age was therefore indeterminate, my clothes appalling, but I exuded drab efficiency. The go-between, happy that I passed muster, offered a pessimistic blessing and my fare to the highlands.

Now I surfaced cautiously. Already I had passed the point of no return and Glenshael really lay ahead of me. I'd gone completely crazy. What, after all, remained of Aillie Rannoch except my sadness for her? A decade dead, the girl who had been me.

The whistle blew. We were away, rattling through built-up areas, headed northwest. Too late to turn and run, but I must keep my wits about me, now and always.

Introspection, then, would be far too unnerving. Wiser to entertain myself by playing sleuth and studying others. The gentleman across the way was not uninteresting. I'd catalogue him.

Late thirties, early forties—hard to judge. He could be younger than he looked. Those lines of discomfort, or merely discontent, were etched quite superficially. I compared him to an actor, made up for some older part with convention but not enough discretion. No good producer would allow raven-black hair against twin silver wings, placed with startling symmetry. It was attractive but a thought amusing. He was a sort of magpie.

I continued to stare at him for he was reading, and I'd

not be the first woman to have done so. Any maternal heart might momentarily throb over his fragile slenderness and biscuit pallor. He needed coddling, building up, and would give precious little thanks for it. I guessed he was ill-humoured and exacting. How long since he last smiled? His mouth was firm, yet grim, and no laughter lurked in the fine lines round his eyes.

Expensive suit, great lack of ostentation, a man born sure of all material things. Yet life, I thought, had rattled him considerably, leaving a lack of happiness or hope. I felt a sudden kinship with him, which gave me little pleasure.

Masked? Yes indeed. Why was I conscious of a different being chained inside him? Curious impression, almost dangerous. I must pass on to the next subject.

The girl was a romantic heroine, another piece of typecasting. Dewy and immaturely pretty, with wide eyes and parted lips, she had a sheltered air of great expectancy. I saw a young imago, newly from the chrysalis with frail wings outspread in search of sunlight. It was a stage I myself had by-passed with no pause to dry out in the gentle breeze. Looking at this child now, I was grateful. Quite horrifying to be so prone to disenchantment.

I was growing cynical. Some people, after all, are born lucky. Girl might meet boy, the path of love run smooth, and everyone be happy ever after.

Meanwhile I found her awkward to place socially. Her clothes and luggage, all quite new, had probably come from a chain store. This wild burst of preholiday extravagance showed one omission. Her shoes were old, well worn, and I was sure they'd been designed for her. I could even guess where they'd originated, which proved that they were shockingly expensive.

There might be several explanations. Still—it was odd. Odd as her taste in literature. Henry Miller at his most tropical. I couldn't think the person that she represented would have chosen such a book. It argued some rebellion or pretension.

Checkmate again. It always happens. On, then, to the last man. Here I controlled a smile. I had not fully taken in his splendour.

He wore elaborate highland dress—kilt, doublet, hose, and sporran. Antlers for his buttons, a cairngorm here and there, a *sgian dubh* at the ready in his stocking. He'd have looked fine in Edinburgh or some such place. You thought he'd soon burst into song about bonnie lassies in the heather.

I tried to cast him as romantic hero; he had the makings of one certainly. I couldn't fault his features or his build; indeed you see the type in women's magazines, which might be why he seemed familiar. Very familiar. It took a moment to remember. I had run across the man before, that very day. He had travelled on the same airplane, wearing a dark town suit. His transformation was remarkable. He'd changed completely. Then he'd been languid as he made excellent progress with a stage-struck girl. I'd heard scraps of their conversation. I wondered if he'd now repeat his tactics, fancying, quite correctly, I would not have long to wait.

"Would my pipe worry you?" he asked the heroine politely. Needless to say, I was not consulted.

"Your pipe? Oh, no!" She blushed prettily, and I noted that her voice, like her shoes, recalled young Mayfair.

"Are you quite sure? Perhaps I could open the window for you slightly?"

"Absolutely not. It's raining far too hard. Besides, I smoke myself—really."

A simple child. She didn't even know it was a lead. Out came the silver cigarette case, the efficient lighter, and he went in to attack. It was done with an engaging diffidence which takes many years of high self-confidence to master. A slick young man . . . I felt uneasy. Had no one ever warned her not to pick up males in trains? I didn't care for boyish smiles mixed up with such hard, shrewd eyes.

"I do hope it clears," she went on less stiltedly. "I've never travelled on this line before but I've heard the scenery's glorious."

"We're not far out of Glasgow which is often murky. There's not much to see at present anyway."

"Do you think it will be better further north? Of course, it's early yet for holidays in Scotland."

"Not really. I usually choose this time of year. It's sometimes warmer than the south, with any luck."

"Well, it was perishing in Glasgow. I'm afraid I found it a dismal city."

"Some parts are better. Take Bearsden, for instance, where I've been staying the last day or so. My aunt there married into shipping, so of course they roll in money. I think if you saw her house and grounds you might change your opinion. I always break my journey to the north."

And he at London airport that same morning!

This gratuitous lie alerted me. Atmospheric, of course, like his dress. Anyhow, why had he changed from top to toe? It had taken all my time to catch this train. I momentarily wondered if I'd been mistaken; if not, the

plot was getting interesting. The paperback by James
Bywater could stay where it was. Real life had more to
offer.

"You'll be a Scot yourself?" the girl was saying. In that
rig-out, he could scarcely admit otherwise.

"I am indeed." He rang with Caledonian pride. I had
my doubts. He wore an Englishness, not a rugged aura of
the tougher north. An accent can be modified but not the
stable look.

"Fabulous country," said the girl.

"I think so, of course. But then I was born and bred
above the highland line. I now have to work in London,
unfortunately, and content myself with one short holiday
a year."

"You don't like London?"

"Off and on. The trouble is I'm essentially an open-air
enthusiast. Only really at home on the grouse moors, or
with my fishing rod in hand. Rather expensive hobbies for
the Home Counties, and you can't stalk deer in Lombard
Street."

"Is that where you work?"

"Yes, I'm a merchant banker, or to be precise, my uncle
is. He's taken me in with him to help repair the family
fortunes. I have to work my way up, of course—he's a
tough old boy—but it means I do have decent prospects."

He was far too fond of relatives, who always seemed to
let him down. Uncle was fiction too. He had told the
young woman on the airplane he worked at Lime Grove
and had great influence in television. It was for this
reason I had carefully kept out of his view. I might have
saved myself the trouble. This was a young man who told

girls exactly what they wished to hear, and did so very thoroughly.

Now he selected Lombard Street to tie up with money and security. Play twopence-coloured hielandman, yet link with London. I thought him just a bit too clever.

Not wishing to appear overattentive, I decided to return to sourpuss, whose elegant nose, down-curved and satisfying, was still buried in his book. I like distinctive features. The merchant banker's were too small and blurred. Pity my neighbour had such a bleak expression, but you can't have everything. At least he was most unlikely to seduce green girls.

*Flowers of the Amazon,* I read upside down. What a wonderfully defiant choice of subject matter! Out the window gaunt pines clung precariously to crag and moor, while cotton grass mapped out the bogland. The highlands were above, about, below, yet joy was still eluding me. Diarlich Moor! A wild, dreich place that's only fit for mountain sheep.

"Less foggy," said the girl. "Do look at that view! Typically Scottish. Absolutely marvellous."

I sighed for her. They crop up all the time, these glamoured southrons. No matter that their holidays are all wet feet, downpours, and mountain mists, they come back for more punishment. You can't dissuade them. They quest for the simple life, the noble savage. It's an incurable infliction.

"You've been up here before?" the young man asked.

"Only by car. A superb grand tour, but of course we never stopped long enough at the best places. I've always promised myself this return. I made a note of Stranach Ferry. Heavenly scenery for miles and miles. A hotel too—the real thing—I'm staying there for two whole weeks."

"Not at the Stranach Hotel?"

"You know it?"

"Good Lord, yes. I've booked there as well. But how extraordinary!"

"What a coincidence! But then, so far north, I suppose it really *is* a small world. There can't be many places open. What fun to find a fellow guest."

I too had planned to overnight in Stranach. We seemed bound up together. And just as well; these two were very entertaining and would provide diversion for the evening. My real thoughts could be kept at bay till the last stage of my journey was upon me. The longer I put them off, the better.

"You've no idea how pleased I am," the boy was saying. "There's a dearth of people of one's own age and type at Stranach. I know; I've stayed there before. It can be deadly in the evenings. In wet weather too—though I fish, of course. Do you, by the way? It's a good center for both trout and salmon."

"I've never tried."

"I could teach you," he said eagerly. "But heavens! What must you think of me? Damned cheek! All I mean is, I'd love to, if you'd like it. Alternatively, if you are bored, we could join up for the occasional drink, or do a film together."

"I'd adore to." She laughed, well pleased at his confusion. "Please don't apologize. I was getting scared, to tell the truth. You see, I've never been on holiday alone before, and I did wonder if there'd be anyone *possible* to

talk to. I'm determined to do a lot of walking in the
daytime, but I was worried about the evenings."

"I'm a walker too, especially in my native mountains. I
belong to the area. Our tribal country is a little south of
Stranach Ferry. Glenshael, to be exact. I wonder if you
know it?"

Was this another lie? If not, who could he be? He
came roughly in my age group, and I was twenty-six. But
suppose he spoke the truth . . . ? The garage boys were
all red-haired. No sign of the loose mouth of the hill
families. Bred in Glenshael! I'd know him surely. Gair,
Grant, McNichol . . . Hector Rannoch? Could he be
Willie-with-the-spectacles who went to live in Glasgow?
Much the same looks as Tam McQueen, but he, poor
laddie, died.

"Our clan territory stretches to Loch Carne," I heard
the young man say. "Which reminds me, it's about time
I introduced myself. My name is Peter Rannoch. It won't
mean a thing to you and probably sounds stupid from a
city clerk, but actually I'm Rannoch of Glenshael."

The devil he was! What damned affrontery! My
father's successor? This young cub! Stupid impostor,
when beyond me was certainly the admiral in Dorset, then
Cousin Ranald with three Californian daughters. If he
must dress up and play-act (and who was I to criticize?),
why, in the name of all that's sacred, did he have to
choose the Rannochs?

Oddly enough, I wasn't quite alone in my annoyance.
For the first time the man opposite showed interest in the
couple. I watched him tap each separate finger on his
knee; one, two, three, four, then start again. A language,

almost certainly, of irritation. He summed up the young man and found him wanting. So did I—in veracity.

What a strange preface to my idiotic comeback! I cursed the boy whole-heartedly, for this was jolting me, against my will, back to the old traditional way of thinking. Time was when a usurping chief paid with his head, and serve him right. Or fulfilled the awful prophecies of Mad Margaret, she who was left with one wee grandchild after the wicked slaughter at Culloden.

"Don't think that I'm a landowner," continued the false Rannoch. "The castle and estate were sold to pay the last laird's debts. Actually the old boy killed himself because he couldn't face the music, having never made the remotest attempt to modify his way of life. My branch of the family were more practical, thank heaven! Still, I'm proud of my name. The pity was that there was no entail, so everything was lost."

"What a shame! Still, I expect the title is important. Head of the clan and so on. I've always heard that highlanders are very *trad* and loyal."

"Heavens, yes. I sometimes wonder if I'm failing in my duty. It's bred in the bone. Yet I'm convinced it's better not to interfere at present. Already they resent the London plutocrat who dares to live at Castle Rannoch. He thinks he's bought the right to stand in Glenshael's place, but no one else does. You know the sort of person. Can't understand my people will never be his servants. To them, of course, he's a foreigner, a parvenu, and far more vulgar than the lowest clansman. They hate him, not surprisingly."

"How ghastly for them."

"You can imagine the situation."

For the first time *I* tried to do so, without success. I had conscientiously ignored the fate of Castle Rannoch. I had no wish to visualize the folk who occupied my home, who walked my glen, and even fished my river. When I allowed myself to speculate upon their mere existence, I vested them with every sort of shortcoming. Mostly, however, I had found oblivion best. Only by putting Glenshael out of mind, by concentrating feverishly on new places, different interests, could I make life attractive, worth the living. Now I had thrown my manufactured world away.

It was a bad mistake, this weak collapse. Subconsciously I'd known it all along. Damn it! Did I *want* to suffer?

Ten years were not enough. I needed twenty more. The half-healed wounds were opening once again. Moreover, they still hurt—they hurt like hell. Absurd! A slow fear came that they might never heal.

All this because of Mister Peter Rannoch. I could have throttled him!

# 2

## The De'il Amang the Tailors

Scene Two: the same, and for hours yet.

When I came home from my school in the south, the journey would seem to last forever. But in those days at least I could anticipate. Would Father meet me in his grand new car? Or send old Angus with the Land Rover? I'd miss the evening rise for sure, but never mind. Tomorrow and tomorrow for a month or more. The Shael was waiting.

Morag would make a layer cake; a special treat on my return. Libby had five more kittens for inspection. Nurse would scold something terrible about my hair. Well, whose head was it? I liked my curly crop. I could keep it tidy now, at any rate. Miss Lamont needn't say I'd left the brush in it. I'd show her after tea. I knew she'd laugh. I liked showing things to Miss Lamont.

After the castle, Holly Bank was fine and cosy, full of dainty, interesting things, and quiet like its owner. I had not then seen Whistler's mother, but when I did I smiled to find such challenging repose and that familiar calm I knew so well.

She was my favourite woman in the whole world, Miss Lamont. There never was anyone more civilized. Funny she chose to live among us; we were not her kind. They came from way down near the Border, her family. She called us a pack of Gaels, and me a half-tamed savage. Well, she should know. She had lived everywhere among the most amazing people. To hear her talk was like a travel book. Her dear Papa had been a British consul and those folk go to foreign countries all the time. She could speak seven different languages, play nearly any kind of music, and paint lovely pictures, mostly in water colours.

She died three months before Father, and Holly Bank was sold.

Now I was going there again. I couldn't quite believe it. I would walk, not run, up the front steps, and find, not Miss Lamont but James Bywater, author of *Naked on My Pavement*. That was the future tense. Too late to call myself a fool. Ignore the past, dismiss the future, concentrate on the minute.

My neighbouring couple had been struggling mazed through highland sociology and economics. The girl was anxious to promote Utopian conditions for peasantry without industrial smears to mar the Celtic paradise. At last, however, she abandoned the keen mental struggle.

"Do tell me more about your fascinating ancestors. They must be thrilling."

"Well, picturesque at least. Extraordinary bunch."

"Do you have a sort of jamboree when you go back?"

"Good Lord, no! I avoid publicity of any sort. As I told you, the object is to keep well in the background till the right time comes. It's not a straightforward situation; there's another heir. Are you sure this interests you?"

"Oh, yes!" she breathed, delighted.

"You see, the old man had a daughter, Alison. Females inherit provided there's no son. But after Glenshael died, the girl disappeared. They hunted high and low but never found a trace of her. She was sixteen at the time and is still officially a missing person ten years after. She had little or no money, she left no clues behind, and that's all anybody knows."

"So she could be dead?"

"It's thought that like the laird, she committed suicide. Not that there's any proof. It's possible. Apart from money difficulties, there was unsavoury local scandal, and Rannochs are pathologically proud. Old Glenshael was a great womanizer and quite without discretion. He pushed the village loyalties a bit too far. Aillie, the girl, certainly blamed the local people for his death. It sounds absurd in this day and age, but she actually stood up at the funeral feast and cursed them in the Gaelic. Whether they understood the lingo or not, they all got the message. It was a nine days' wonder."

"Peter, how legendary!" She blushed belatedly at this new boldness. "I hope you don't mind if I call you that? I'm vague about forms of address to highland chieftains. And I, by the way, am Diana Marston—shop assistant in the West End, quite deadly dull."

"Believe me, I don't find you dull, Diana."

"But I am," she protested. "I haven't even got a family. Not any more. I live with a sort of cousin."

I pulled my roving thoughts back to her, wishing she weren't an orphan. Intrusive mothers and stern fathers have their uses. Or was I overprejudiced? My pseudo-cousin might be a romancer but this did not imply real harm in him. His lies amused me. It was only when he spoke the truth that I awoke, not only to distrust, but something near to hatred.

That he should laugh about what happened! What a thing to discuss in a railway train. I daren't remember it myself. Never . . . never . . . all those years in London.

"Go on about your rival," said Diana. "What do you think happened?"

He shrugged. "The locals believe she returned to drown herself in the river Shael."

"But they'd find the body. . . ."

"Not necessarily. Some of the upper parts are deep and inaccessible. Mountain gorges and so on. However, that is not the point. She doesn't rest in peace. She moves around and curses everyone she meets. No villager will go near the river or the glen at the full moon. She haunts the place and worries them to death. Highlanders have very active imaginations and are proud of them. They say that Aillie Rannoch *walks,* and while she does they persist in regarding her as their hereditary chief."

"Not logical. The fact they believe she's dead should make them accept you more readily."

"That's too easy. You don't know them. They rather like their ghost and don't wish to frighten her away."

Would this be fact or fiction? Me, a ghost! The Teen-

age Specter of Glenshael! Not only funny but convenient.
You don't look for the living *and* the dead. To focus on a
phantom means ignoring the substance. It could be an
excellent protection, a piece of luck. Not that I had too
many qualms. I'd been an actress—quite a good one.
Child's play to suit James Bywater's requirements. The
village folk would note the spinsterish air, the London
accent, and the smug gentility. Ten years were added to
my age; I even wore a faded, mousy wig for extra safety.
I hardly recognized myself. Nothing was left of sixteen-
year-old Aillie.

The secret is to live a part through and through. Miss
Alice Rayner, typist, was reality; that half-baked highland child was dead indeed. Impossible to remember how
it felt to have her tireless energy, her stormy heart, her
wild cockeyed viewpoints. Yes, she had cursed them, and
she'd meant each Gaelic word she said. Miss Rayner
could not visualize such odd extravagance.

Love curdled, pain articulate, a world blighted. First
Nurse, then Miss Lamont, then Father. It was a dreadful
year.

"Which makes things difficult for me," continued the
false Rannoch. "One day I hope to be accepted, even by
the Lord Lyon King of Arms. But I confess I'd like to do
it properly. I'm not impractical. Get back the land and
Castle Rannoch first. A splendid investment, incidentally; even my uncle says so. It's a tall order but I'm
saving hard already, and my branch of the family will
help. Meanwhile I don't want to upset people till I'm
ready. A coup d'état, in fact."

"I see. But what about the present owner?"

"He seems to be an invalid with one foot in the grave. I

only hope he lasts out till the time comes. It's lucky actually. He's elderly and ill, unmarried with no obvious heirs, and they're nearly sure to sell up when he dies. A complete dead loss, in fact. No one will even miss him."

This display of very questionable taste alerted sour-puss. He turned his head towards the boy with a curious expression on his face. I thought I saw a trace of wry amusement and certainly scorn. Then he proceeded to Diana.

I watched him. One eyebrow up, the other down, a new tattoo upon his knee. Sourpuss was puzzled, and no wonder. A man might find it difficult to realize moonshine could so deceive her. And of course, Peter's style was all wrong. No ring of the true coin about my pseudo-cousin. To anyone who knew the highlands he'd be counterfeit.

My neighbour had not finished. I too was included. Once started he was thorough. I looked out the window quickly. I must condition myself to careful scrutiny; call this a trial run. Compose the face, relax each separate muscle, keep the hands still. Not so easy. His stare set up some physical compulsion I could not control. Or was it merely nerves which made my heart beat faster?

He pulled me in a queer way; I had to look at him. Gray eyes: not light, yet not so dark as you'd expect. They met mine momentarily with cool impertinence. I glared haughtily till he went back to his book.

I'm reasonably honest with myself when it's possible. Besides it amused me to admit I wished to look different. I longed suddenly to throw off my quaint disguise and cause more gratifying symptoms. If it had been before my accident . . . but no use thinking of it. Funny how vanity plagues those least entitled to it. I was in no position to give way to such nonsense. I hoped the man would disappear at Fort John. I'd had enough of him.

Sometimes one detrains there, sometimes not. On that day I was unlucky. We switched engines only, taking on two small ones for the lower bridges. My Cousin Rannoch dashed out gallantly to fetch two cups of tea. The magpie gentleman recrossed his legs and changed to *The Financial Times*. I contemplated moving all my luggage and then shrugged. Who were these people anyway? Mere shadow-players. We steamed out of Fort John still a foursome.

Our pace was spanking. My very thoughts accelerated. From now on I could happily dismiss the three of them. Each landmark had its name and every name its own secret. That croft belonged to the McGilvrays; there was the cottage where the triplets lived; the English artist lady at Fairbrae still kept those foreign goats with spaniel's ears. Glenwilly, Achinfaa, to Dousie Bridge. Did old Sir Hector still drink like a fish? He must be over eighty now, the creature, if he were still alive. Nurse said that he was heading for delirium tremens.

Clachan and market town; the sleepy stations and the wayside halts; through strath and moor, by glen and forest; all wonderfully familiar. The hills too, with their older, Gaelic names. I knew them all.

We swept down to Loch Carne, gold-fringed with seaweed, a fine, watery lever to thrust Scotland apart. Then up again, a thousand feet or more, where wet turf, sparkling with white flowers, lurked in the dour gray crags like emerald in matrix. Higher and higher, poor wee train. The mist now wrapped it like a blanket. Nothing to see but long trickles down the windowpane. Damn the cloud!

We must emerge . . . we *must*. Downhill now . . . down . . . to home!

It cleared at last; and there below us, Stranach Ferry, a white toy-town, cosy beside the water. How beautiful and neat!

It was like going home in the old days, and I wild with excitement. Geordie Cameron would ring his wee bells while Father checked the time on his gold hunter. He never wore a wrist watch, Father. I could hear him after all these years.

"Ach, Aillie, you have grown again, I'm thinking. Your skirts are something less than decent. Stop jumping up and down like a wee dog. Have you your ticket? Well, Geordie, here's the terror of St. Trinian's. Would you believe it—I spend good money on that uniform? Willie can stow her luggage in the car. I'll be at Mrs. Morrison's. Come on, you young limb of Satan, and I'll stand you a drink. I badly need a dram myself. It's bleak weather."

"Could I have a Coke, Father?"

"And take the enamel off your teeth? What would Mrs. Wilson say? Still, it's your first day home. We'll see."

He'd go into the bar while I sat in the lounge and read *The Scottish Field*. Then I'd grow bored and stare through the lace curtains at the street. People, real Stranach people. It was good to see them. Were they not lucky to be there all the time and never go away except for funerals? Education was a strange thing forbye. You have to have it—everybody said so. But why must I go down to England, wasting good time in foreign places? Robin said it was so I could be a spy when we next fought the English. He was a few years older and a tease.

"A spy? Would any Rannoch sink so low? I mean to fight. Am I not fine and handy with a gun?"

"A gun? Would you not use a claymore?"

"I would not. I'll leave you to brandish one, and a grand mess you'll make of it."

"But Aillie, you're a female. You'll need to stay at home to grow food for the menfolk."

"I shall not!"

"Knit stockings and sew brogues, I'm thinking. A ministering angel you will be for sure."

"I'll not be ministering to you, Anacher, I'll tell you that! The idea of it. Ach, let go my hair, Robin, it hurts. I think I'll practice for my wars on you."

"Aillie, behave yourself! It's a wee wildcat you are, and all your good English education thrown away on you."

"It is not! I can talk like those ones if I wish. *Isn't the whether ghastly? Don't you adore the Highlands? Are you Scottish, Mister Macdonald?*"

Nurse said I ought to speak like that myself. She was a great one to know about *ladies*, Nurse. What they did and what they didn't. The idea was, I should grow into one. I could laugh to think of it.

Robin did. He really was a cousin of sorts—several removes at once. In the old days, when our families were not fighting one another, we'd intermarry—blood ties to save blood feuds. Then, too, I don't suppose they could know many people before the trains and suchlike. The Macdonalds of Anacher were fine and handy, and the boundaries of our land and influence had always marched together. Nurse, who was wont to choose me a new husband every week, mostly returned to Robin. She was fond of tradition for tradition's sake, like everyone I knew.

"Anacher? Ach, away! Would I be marrying him? He would drive me daft in no time. Anyone would be better almost. I'll tell you, Nurse, if I *wish* to be married, I'll find myself a husband when I'm ready. A fine rich Englishman, the sort who stay in the big houses for the shooting. He'll buy me diamond rings and Paris frocks, and I shall keep three wee dogs on a string, with jewels in their collars."

"Is it likely such a one would take you? And if it's diamond rings you're wanting, you'd best stop biting your nails straightaway, or more likely you'll be wearing gloves to cover up your fingers, like your poor Auntie Johann who was drowned."

Nurse could turn any conversation to correction, and all her similes had doom-struck ends.

Poor tenuous spirits, dead these many years, no longer waiting for me. But was that true? I felt them somehow. And what of Robin? Slight panic gained on me. The train was gliding into Stranach station. I must concentrate. Transfer the luggage to the platform, adjust my horrid hat, call Geordie's Willie "Porter"—do things properly. I was an incomer who did not know my way around. I asked for the Hotel, not Mrs. Morrison's.

I lost sight of my travelling companions, all except Peter, who helped me to pass through the barrier unobserved, there was such a fuss about his ticket. I heard him say he'd changed his mind and wouldn't go on to the Kyle. Nor did he want a refund. You could see he gave a very bad impression. They don't like waste in Stranach.

An opportunist, the false Rannoch, and as glib a liar as I'd ever met. Yet I felt for him, momentarily, an almost cousinly affection and something near to gratitude. When I had need of outside interest, when uncontrollable nostalgia was halfway up my throat, he turned up like a bad coin to divert me; and I used him, much as he used others, though perhaps for better reasons.

Aware now that my pilgrimage was sad and frightening, and I made it with no scallop shell of quiet at all.

# 3

## Ladies' Fancy

A BRIEF GLANCE round the lounge and I avoided it. The dark varnish, the huge steel engravings, the tattered dog-eared magazines had mouldered just one more decade. Even the curtains, heavy olive plush, had lost only a few more bobbles in the years. The moon-face clock was still slow.

The bar, however, had completely changed, and very rich and strange it was. I could no longer imagine Father, dram in hand. He'd hardly lean against a plastic curve or twist his legs round bare chromium. Strip lighting shone benignly upon shelves filled with liqueurs; a spray of flowers, after Constance Spry, was isolated in a special niche. As for the walls, you never saw the like. They were panelled in assorted tartans. Pure Balmoral.

The local folk, I knew, would jib at all this tourist splendour and prefer the public bar behind. Such stragglers as were here seemed deep in conversation. Only one sat apart, a girl with witching eyes. Her pointed face and shy smile put me in mind of a picture we once had at home of one of the *daoine sidhe,* the fairy folk, their queen perhaps, thrusting a most reluctant mortal through the hillside. This girl had the same beckoning way with her. I ought to have known better right enough. Nurse said that you must never speak to the Good People, but I was tired of playing deaf-mute and chose the table next to her.

She smiled a sort of understanding welcome.

"How is the weather getting on?" She had a very English voice.

"Clearing, I think. It's better here than further south."

"I suppose you're on holiday?"

"Far from it. I'm here to work, not gallivant. This is my last night of freedom."

"Does talking to you spoil it? I should apologize. I hate sitting in bars alone; it makes me madly sociable and chatty and often unintentionally inquisitive. So you've come up here to take a job? Usually it's the reverse process. Do you go further north?"

"South—to Glenshael."

"Good gracious! You must be James Bywater's new secretary. I'd forgotten the advertisement was in *The Times* again. I really shouldn't say this, but his requirements always sound so formidable. Hermits and old-age pensioners only need apply. How brave you are!"

"I'm beginning to think so—especially as I've never lived in before. Are you on holiday yourself?"

"No, I'm a part-time resident nowadays. But I first came up here on a job too, so I know exactly how you feel. I was terrified. I'd never even met my employer."

"Nor have I. What's he like?"

"I don't really know him—seen him, of course, in Stranach, and as one exile to another I smirk suitably. He doesn't seem to blend at all. Doesn't want to. You know the type—very high above the philistines and rude peasantry. They say he's a good novelist and his prose is deathless, as prose goes. Me, I prefer Jane Austen."

"His books don't give a picture of a domestic pet. I gather he's a bachelor. A gay one?"

"In Glenshael? How could he be? It's not that sort of place. Mind you, they watch him there like hungry lynxes, on the off-chance that he will oblige. But I shouldn't think there was much smoke and certainly no fire. He's a type born middle-aged."

"Sounds rather dull."

"Well, that's better than the other thing," she assured me.

We had another drink and gossiped leisurely. I had forgotten the lack of hustle in the Highlands; it soothed me like a benediction.

"And how about Glenshael itself?" I might as well pick her brains. "A young man on the train was telling ghost stories about it to a girl he had picked up. I listened avidly, of course, but it was too far-fetched."

"Ghosts are Glenshael's speciality. It hotches with them. Did you hear about Mad Margaret on her rock? And the volatile, ubiquitous Aillie Rannoch? Glenshael—well, if you like scenic splendour and variety, there it is. Just the same, I find it has a weird atmosphere. Why, I don't know. It's more open and sunny than my home, Anacher. The people too are more assorted. And yet it has a blighted air."

I did not fully take this in. Anacher! Not many people lived there certainly, and few of them belonged to her type. I'd better find out at once who she was.

"You live at Kinlochanacher?"

"Miles from that outpost even. A house called Ilsafeccan. I don't mind the remoteness, never get too much of it. We have a flat in Edinburgh as well, but while the children are preschool we can and do make long stays. I'm what my husband calls a heather hunter and not ashamed of it. I bask in Celtic twilight. He, of course, is the local laird. The name's Macdonald, by the way—very much of Anacher. What's yours?"

"Alice Rayner," I returned absently, my thoughts in tumult. Of all the women in the world, I had to pick Robin's wife! I'd gambled on my sharp-eyed cousin's absence, but now it seemed I might run into him—the last person to see Aillie Rannoch living! I'd pushed his memory from me.

From Glasgow onwards I had carefully suppressed that other railway train which headed south.

I was sixteen, lumpish in my school uniform. My hands were grubbier and far more restless. I'd left my home; I'd never see Glenshael again. My eyes were heavy, not through crying but the lack of it. Empty; I could feel the hollowness. They'd taken all I valued, all I loved. It wasn't worth existing any more.

Across the way sat Robin with a tome on engineering. He's promised Aunt Ishbel he would see me across Glasgow. She seemed to think I would be coshed or murdered. Silly old bitch! She ought to be damned glad to see the

last of me. Already she'd begun to grin and grouse about
my school fees. Well, she needn't think I'd live with her
and be a day girl. Edinburgh was a dirty place. The grit
blew off the streets into your nose and eyes. Imagine
coming back each day up the dark stair which led to her
airless, cluttered flat; for company her yawling foreign
cats and Uncle Archie's ectoplasm. How could I possibly
depend on her and be a piece of charity? I'd rather die.

The full circle again. Death was necessary. It was required of me—Father too—so who was I to argue?
They'd all turned against us; I shared his burden and his
shame. I had no friends, no home, no heritage—a beggar
with no pride left at all. No place to go, and no one to
belong to. What was the use of living anyway?

But I wouldn't shoot myself. I couldn't. It was a
shocking thing to do.

"Our loved ones leave us for a happier land," said Aunt
Ishbel. "Your dear father wouldn't wish you to grieve. He
has passed over to a better place."

Old hypocrite! *Dear father. . .* ! They'd fought like cat
and dog. He couldn't stand her either.

"I'll be away upstairs."

"No, my dear child. There's no necessity. His astral
body is no longer with us."

She was a spiritualist, Aunt Ishbel, and Uncle Archie
wrote her messages saying that he was very joyful there
across the way. Father suggested there must be whisky,
women, and some trout fishing, if he knew Archie Menzies, or he'd not be so uncommon pleased with after-life.
Now it seemed wrong to laugh about such things.

"Nevertheless," I said, "I must go to him."

"I forbid it, Alison. You've no idea . . . Dr. Morrison was adamant. The gun, he said, was fired—well—rather close."

"I know that fine. What difference does it make?"

"You're tired, my dear, after that long journey—and why you have to go so far afield to school, I can't imagine—if I'd had my way, you wouldn't have come back to this sad tragedy at all. It's most unsuitable."

"But no concern of yours, Aunt Ishbel. You are no Rannoch of Glenshael. Nor of my blood—my mother's brother's wife. Naturally I come home at such a time. We have our customs and we understand them. One is to pay a decent tribute to our dead."

"My dear Alison, there's no need to strike such attitudes. But I must forgive you your rudeness. This dreadful accident is too much of a shock."

"Accident? I think not. They drove him to it. His own people killed him—and they'll pay. He's dead; that's final. I can't bring him back. But I'll see the murderers know whose fault it was."

"You're ridiculous, Alison! We don't want more scandal than we have."

"Dishonour, do you mean? An old-fashioned word. We have it right enough and can't escape it. A little more or less scarcely matters. Where is McDhui?"

"That horrible old man! I told him to keep out of this part of the house. He reeks of whisky."

"This is my house, Lady Menzies. I say who comes and goes. Though I have bought the honour dear, I am Glenshael from this time on. I will send for McDhui. It is right he alone should take me to my father. The two were lifelong friends and his distress is deep and genuine, and

you will not upset him further. We may adopt some
lowland ways, but this is not the time for them."

She'd have gone on and on, that woman, but I could
not wait to listen. Angus McDhui stood there in the hall.
We didn't exchange words at all. He bowed to me, came
like a dog to heel, and we went up the long stair together.

A shutter seemed to click in my mind. I shook myself
and looked about me. A bar, a young woman . . .
Robin's wife, of course! I had forgotten her completely.

She would think me most eccentric—or did these flash-
backs time like a dream? Nevertheless, I'd better find
some quiet, innocuous subject of conversation. But what?

At this juncture, like a conjuring trick, Diana Marston
and her escort walked into the room. A useful couple!

"There's my folklore expert and his young woman. We
travelled up together."

"Lord! What a Monarch of the Glen!"

"That's the whole point. He was on my plane as well,
but looking very different. To change from head to foot
just for the Highland Line appears to argue some extreme
of patriotism."

"She's pretty, isn't she? And very radiant. Madly in
love with him, I'd say, and I'm a judge. Are they both
staying here?"

"Unfortunately, yes. She meant to all along; he dove-
tailed in." I gave her a brief outline of events, quite
grateful to discuss them.

"Love at first sight." She smiled. "More common than
you'd think. I hope he gets her, bless him. I'm anti-
laggard, all for Lochinvar."

"What grade of love? Does this, I ask myself, stop short of the hotel bedroom door?"

"You read too many novels by James Bywater. That girl, I'm sure, is very *bien élevée*. Innocence is its own protection, so they say."

"I doubt it. Anyway not with him. He's not her type, and I've never met a more accomplished liar."

I continued to elaborate, including a dissertation on clan leadership. My companion gulped it down.

"It's not impossible," she said when I had finished. "I've often thought that girl may have died. It stands to reason. Take my husband—he could never keep away from Anacher for ten years without even communicating. He is convinced Aillie will turn up somewhere, probably as the first female prime minister of Great Britain. I disagree."

"Well, Peter Rannoch is of your persuasion. He likes killing people off. He soon hopes to bury the ancient, moribund incumbent of Castle Rannoch so he can buy the estate and become your country neighbour."

"What fun! It should be lively. A change from Alastair. Did you call him moribund and elderly, by the way? He's not exactly old, and I thought he looked much better when I last saw him. He'll live for years yet, mark my words."

"You mean the vulgar English plutocrat who isn't capable of tilling Rannoch soil?"

"As to that, the Monarch is a bit sweeping. Alastair is a notable landlord. He even makes money out of that estate, which is more than the Rannochs ever did. Nor would I call him vulgar. And though he has an English finish certainly, he's all Gael within—the gloomy, melancholy sort. He personifies Glenshael, in fact. Most suitable."

"I can see this place is full of weird attractions."

"Don't count on Alastair. You won't run across him much. He keeps the village at arm's length and plays the anchorite. He hates the human race, our Mr. Forres, and women more than most. I only know him myself because he and Robin belong to the same club, which means we must exchange meals once or twice a year. I shall never understand men. They cultivate such dull allegiances."

"Is it this man's gloom which affects Glenshael?"

"No, for they wouldn't shift their loyalties in any case. Rannochs or nothing is their motto, whatever their opinion. Alastair Forres demands nothing but efficiency and pays for it well. In a negative way he suits them admirably."

I understood what she meant. They would rather hate a Rannoch than love some strange outsider. Forres sounded an east coast name forbye.

"To return to my heroine," I said firmly. "She soaks tradition up like blotting paper. She's the type who comes in search of peace and primitive simplicity, and what she's found is Mr. Rannoch, who's about as simple as a Sunday crossword. I wouldn't be in her shoes, expensive though they are."

"Put like that, it does seem wrong. Ought we to do something?"

I shrugged. "Why on earth? Two complete strangers? Hardly our affair."

"I don't like to think of anyone who's gullible and quite alone. I've been that way myself. I was a romantic too; still am, really. I feel responsible. Are you sure you're not exaggerating? After all, you're only guessing."

She frowned at me, her queries clearly written in her eyes. No doubt I seemed a most unlikely judge of men. My current image was misleading, hardly allowing for a mild flirtation with a curate. However, I had said too much already, though she had given fair exchange.

I smiled back placidly, and suddenly she pricked up and I watched her face light up to beauty. I did not have to turn my head. The voice was only too familiar. It trapped me.

"My love, I'm abject. Have you been waiting hours? I tried to get away earlier, but he went on and on. Are you starving? I am. Can't we eat here?"

"I was going to suggest it. The kids are at the Farm. I knew you'd get held up with old Sir Hector. How is he?"

"Better. He'll live to be a hundred. I did try to telephone."

"Forget the apologies. I've enjoyed myself. I've been having a long talk with Miss Rayner here. She's James Bywater's new secretary. I've been telling her all about Glenshael, which she has never seen."

He smiled perfunctorily and looked me up and down. I think I held my breath. No flicker there of recognition and quite a lot of boredom. My spirits rose. I'd passed my preliminary, and if I could deceive Robin, the future looked much safer.

"Mrs. Macdonald has been so helpful," I said brightly.

"And Miss Rayner fascinating. She's been telling me, Robin, that boy up by the bar is the new Rannoch of Glenshael. The one wearing the kilt."

"Who said?"

"He does," I put in smoothly. "I overheard him."

"Rubbish! In Campbell tartan? Be there a Rannoch with a soul so dead, what with the Forty-Five and Margaret's granddaughter."

The matter, being thus disposed of to his satisfaction, he took the chair between us and finished off his wife's martini.

"But Robin," she persisted, "he comes from London. He might not know."

"My dear Catherine, exiles are more punctilious than the people on the spot. Look at the folk in Edinburgh. They make a cult of it. Besides, Glenshael is female gender. The admiral won't bother now, and Ranald's gone. If Aillie doesn't turn up, we'll get the Californians. No, love, this is imposture. It stands out a mile. He looks a crook anyhow. He's very like that steward on the boat."

"Robin, you're right! And women fell for him too. He got three years, Miss Rayner, for robbery and blackmail."

"You're sure it's not the same man?" I asked.

"No, but the same type. I don't like him any more."

"Did you ever?" Robin was amused. "He seems a little overdressed, if I may say so."

It was impossible to extricate myself while Catherine represented the position with frequent appeals to me for confirmation. I used the opportunity, however, for digestion. I hadn't known Robin had married until that evening, and now it seemed he had a family. More cousins. I would like to see them. They would be bonnie bairns for Macdonalds bred true. Lucky for Anacher. Glenshael sounded barren.

"Ach, love, what tales you tell!" Robin was laughing. "However, if the Fause Rannoch is as cool as he looks, I doubt if he'll try and spread his gospel locally. And if he does, old Angus will gun him, that's for sure."

"Robin, couldn't you get into conversation with them and prick the Rannoch bubble at least?"

"My dear girl, with all due deference to your strange social tastes, there is a limit, and that exceeds it. It's not my business to interfere with tourists' ploys or advise them on their methods of seduction."

He hadn't changed, my cousin Anacher. High in the instep, Father called him. And not exactly tactful, when you thought of Dear Miss Rayner. I'd have liked fine to have heard what he said about me afterwards. Poor Catherine! Nice girl. Presumably she liked her lot. Well, he was even more attractive now he'd put on weight.

Lucky our paths need seldom cross. A brief nod would do if we met in Stranach. But to the best of my ability I would avoid the pair of them. I wanted no unnecessary risks.

# 4

## Cold and Raw

I ATE MY dinner thoughtfully. By the window, the Macdonalds worked through the menu with country relish; to my left, Diana picked at salmon mayonnaise, her eyes fixed on Peter. Too much love in the air. I found myself a little envious.

Not that I'd any cause to grumble. If I'd avoided high romance and charming domesticity alike, I could blame no one but myself. I'd gone my way, cutting life to my pattern. A bit late to wonder what I'd missed, and girn about it. I'd had fun, after all. I'd climbed the pinnacle I'd chosen, and used other people's hearts to save my own.

Now these folk were affecting me, and I knew why. Might as well face it and get it over. Beyond passing attractions, impudent flirtations, loitered my brief first love in that recurring sixteenth year. My stripling cousin had grown smug and settled, but to see him brought it all back. My memory was becoming like a powder train.

Child's play at first. Could he not make a grand cast? And was he not my favourite partner in the reel? Bonnie too. They had an air, the Anachers. Robin could raise his eyebrows very high, till you felt of no importance whatsoever—a thing I didn't like at all. It was necessary to have someone to boast about at school. Who better than my handsome cousin?

But on that last train journey I felt more adult, and anyhow he was the only person I had left to love. I studied him in minute detail. It helped me to forget what must come. If I could kill myself, I must be grown up. Love was one experience I needn't miss by dying young, which is a very sobering thing to do.

Besides, I'd settled every point. There was a railway junction, about halfway, where I could throw myself in front of an express. Anna Karenina. I'd just read the book. Her last thoughts were silly; I could improve on them. I'd think of Robin; far more dignified. His name would be the last word on my lips. In those days I read too many novels and always altered them to my much higher standards.

So I gazed at Robin conscientiously, not just his features but his tricks. I recorded his voice with every small inflection, till I soon knew more about him than he did himself. His hair was rough and curly, and at that time he wore it rather long like Greeks and Romans. He was like that daft emperor who cried because he'd no more worlds to conquer, but Anacher was made of sterner stuff, and as for worlds, you could bet he'd find one somewhere.

"Have I a smut on my nose, puss? Why the solemn stare?"

"I shall not see you any more."

"Idiot child! Next holidays I'll be in Edinburgh and we'll do a cinema or something. Would you like that?"

"Yes, Robin."

"There's loads to do, you know. And by yourself too, now you're older. The country's rather dull really. Cities are fun."

"Yes, Robin."

"Good Lord! You keep agreeing with me! Cheer up, puss. It doesn't suit you to be docile."

I smiled half-heartedly as I probed deeper. He was much thinner since his mother died, looked rather tired and more aloof than ever.

"Robin? Do you like Glasgow? Honest?"

"Not really. I'm damned homesick. But you'll find it doesn't do to hark back. A real upheaval needs a clean break and does no harm. Our sort of roots are very deep; we can't escape them, but that doesn't mean we need grow into stunted vegetables. The world's huge, Aillie— and full of other interests."

"Full of strangers!"

"You mustn't think like that. It's fatal. Escape this deep involvement with home. Otherwise you'll be veering towards every slight connection. It spoils your judgment, and it's dangerous. I've found that out myself. You must push towards new friends, new ambitions, and work like hell for them."

"Substitutes!"

"Not necessarily. Or they may not always stay so."

I did not argue. It seemed pointless. Glenshael or

nothing was my motto. "For God's sake, hold your
tongue and let me love," I might have said. There wasn't
much more time.

He saved my life. Not that I was grateful. The fact
was, I couldn't shake him off. First he said we'd loads of
time, so he took me down to Govan Ferry to see the mist-
bound shipyards with their sad, surrealist crucifixes. I
must say it was interesting. I thought of all the great
boats on the Clyde, sailing off to lands I'd never seen. Not
that I wanted to exactly. Still, they were there—acces-
sible.

I must go through with my intention. . . . I *must!*
But the longer it was postponed, the more wasteful it
seemed. Would I be committing a mortal or a deadly sin?
At any rate, the Almighty was against self-slaughter.

"That was the whistle. You must get off, Robin."

"I have a ticket."

"But—but you were only asked to take me across
Glasgow."

"Nevertheless, I'll go a bit further with you. I have a
friend near your school. I'd like to look him up."

Later I was to wonder if he'd guessed. When that
junction came, he was always at my elbow. It was one
thing to die alone, another to involve a friend in every
sort of unpleasantness. Nor could it be an accident, with
Robin sticking like a leech. They might even say he'd
pushed me. I couldn't do it.

The Rannoch love of melodrama ebbed away reluctantly. I would never know whether I had been mad
with grief or just pigheaded. Then too, I couldn't think of
any other method; my mind wouldn't co-operate. Robin
alone remained reality.

He was most thorough, handing me over to Matron personally. I felt like a wee girl, spared a skelping, and my long dramatic day ended with cocoa. I could have laughed if I'd not been so tired.

"I take it very kindly, Anacher, you should have gone to all this trouble." I robed myself with rags of dignity.

"Come off it, Aillie! Don't strike attitudes."

"I'm grateful, Robin. Honestly."

"That's better. Now smile. You'll be fine now with all your little friends. Work hard, play hard, and try to forget. I know it's been a shocking time, but things will mend, believe me. I'll write if you remind me, and see you in the holidays. Goodbye, love. I must go or that human dragon will skin me alive. Poor puss, don't look so glum."

A cousinly kiss. I cherished it for months, and all the girls peeped through the banisters and whispered. It was goodbye indeed, and I knew it. I hadn't seen him since.

"Everything to your satisfaction, madam?" I looked up and saw Amy Morrison. She had new false teeth.

"Excellent, thank you."

"All our food comes from local sources, I'm glad to say."

"Splendid," I murmured, wondering if she ever thought of Father. They said she'd favoured him even when Alec Morrison was on the scene. Everyone knew too much about each other in these parts. No wonder Father came to grief.

I was sorry I had earned this courtesy, which I owed, I knew, to Catherine Macdonald. A bored impulse on the part of Robin's wife could put me on the social map. I had a patroness, an English girl at that. I almost laughed.

"It is a pity you are only staying one night, I'm thinking."

"I'm a working woman."

"Yes, I have heard you go to Mr. Bywater. I hope that you will like Glenshael, though it's not the place it was without the Rannochs at the castle."

As far as I could judge, I had passed my intermediate. Stupid to be so nervous. It was doubtful if I'd be recognized even without disguise. I'd left here a raw schoolgirl and buried my transition period, and anyhow had aged years since my accident. When I came out of hospital old friends hadn't known me.

They hadn't made a bad job of me at hospital, all things considered. They'd been convinced I'd die, but somehow I pulled through. The trouble was it drained my little store of strength to tackle life again from a new angle, and the way I seemed to swing from importance to nonentity was disconcerting. I was like a damned pendulum. It wore me down.

Amy went away to intercept Robin. The Macdonalds were just leaving. Catherine smiled at me across the room, but my dear cousin ignored me. I was glad that he looked so happy and content.

After he took me back to school, I settled down vaguely. It was, after all, the only haven that I had, a pleasant enough place with its fine trees and sleepy river. No hills; I didn't want them. I was chary of reminders.

The ache continued, but sharp pain receded. I often thought of Robin. My love for him was tangible, as was my hatred for Aunt Ishbel. I wouldn't depend on her; impossible—a woman we had all disliked.

Then the miracle, just to show they happen. They chose me for Mark Antony in the school play.

Me! Mark Antony! I couldn't believe it. After all, I'd only had very small parts before, though I'd enjoyed them. I went around quite translated, right back to life again. Not only did the moderate honour relieve my nothingness, but it supplied me at last with an outlet for my stored emotions.

Now I could be articulate again with no responsibility. *"You all did love him once, not without cause . . ."* Poor, murdered Caesar!

The great day came. I was good, and knew how good I was. Bored parents, anxious staff pricked to enthusiasm. I carried them, via ancient Rome, to mourn at a funeral. My power went out, returned threefold, and had a heady tang at the first taste.

I was an actress. I could move an audience. It was the answer and the future. An object; something to grip hard. I now knew my direction. Not that Mark Antony was quite original. The person I projected was no Roman. That careful scrutiny of my first love had paid dividends. A toga'd Anacher! Love is evidently creative at its most abortive. I consummated mine that summer night.

All indecision left me. No one would stop me this time. Again my junction at the end of term but no death scene. I caught a southbound train and disappeared. And that was that.

It seemed odd, in retrospect, that I should have been successful—one dogged, sixteen-year-old girl against the world. Aunt Ishbel was too slow in calling the police. No doubt she dreaded further scandal. It gave me time to go to earth, a hunted animal with no closed season. A brutal battleground for one so sheltered. Life equalled survival, nothing else. I'd always meant to fight the English but not twentieth-century London, though it proved a well-loved enemy and lost gracefully. Out of the gutter, into the surtax bracket, and no opportunity to brood about Glenshael. I did fine till I found myself in hospital, but then my thoughts wandered and the lost girl sometimes beckoned me and plagued me about home.

Had I come back to reclaim her in a weak moment? To what end? I had grown my carapace and wore it comfortably. Poor Aillie, she'd been warm and loving, amusing, vital, but damned easily hurt. It didn't do to feel deeply. The pole was slippery, and I often hit rock bottom. Life seemed to have some grudge against me. Why play into its hands?

Everything short of death on two occasions, but before new accidents I'd see my home.

I took my book into the shabby lounge. I was alone, save for one asthmatic gentleman who soon fell into snoring sleep. I skimmed through the stark prose of my employer with only part attention. Yet as I retraced the day and all its introductions, it was my sourpuss with the magpie hair who returned most clearly. I had forgotten him in all the bustle of arrival. Had he too alighted? The junction served a good few scattered parishes; it needn't mean we'd meet again. Resident, tourist, travelling on business? I wished belatedly I had cross-examined Catherine to see if she could place him.

I smiled to myself, pleased with my own stupidity. I hadn't fluttered in the pulses since my crash. So this seemed an achievement. I was proud of being nearer normal, enjoying human failings. Come to think of it, I was not very tired either, less so than after a day's work sandwiched between the rush-hour tube trains.

Of course the last thing I wanted was primitive emotion with all its fiendish complications, but my recent neighbour had vanished obligingly. It was therefore permissible to wonder how I *might* have felt. At closer acquaintance could he have been more sociable? It need not, I reflected wryly, demand a noticeably high standard.

Strange that my last thoughts on that day should be of him. I lay back in the dark, inventing a conversation about *Flowers of the Amazon,* but as my ignorance on the subject was total I soon grew bored and drifted off to sleep.

# 5

## Codlen Hame

I AWOKE LIGHT-HEARTED. A good night's rest had toughened me, and I felt confident, having weathered Mrs. Morrison and Robin without disaster. Today I only faced James Bywater, a safe stranger. Besides, Holly Bank stood at the far end of the village where I could keep my distance and ration my adventuring.

It was a clean-washed, golden morning after the rain. The only clouds were wisps of cotton wool which clung to the high tops. I had forgotten that the grass could be so green, the sky so blue. White houses shone in the clear air and all the birds were calling to each other.

The morning bus still left at the same time. The south road. Stranach Ferry safe behind us. Farm meadows first, then we began to climb. The bus, as was its habit always, started to groan and grumble. I didn't recognize the young driver, but I swear the vehicle had not been changed. It had great temperament. First it protested at the gradient, then as we straightened out it tore along in manic jubilation, screaming its tires, pulling up on its haunches, only to leap forward like a greyhound when the way was clear. The wildest bus in the northwest, the creature, with juddering breaks and coughed acceleration. Its passengers had learnt to ride it like a bucking horse—and so had I.

I watched the rowans toppling over rocks, saw with delight the chain of oval moorlochs. This was bog country bright with asphodel and water, a land close to the sky.

It passed. I held my breath. We went over the rim and, there below, my love stretched out before me. The great Sound had the dark shine of old-world silver, Beinn Cullach was as hunched as Caliban; and to the south, our own Stac Liath—feminine, symmetrical, and very lovely. Miss Lamont lived at Holly Bank, she said, to watch her flirting with the clouds. She'd once seen Fujiyama, Miss Lamont, but didn't think it half so beautiful.

How small the village looked! A child had thought it big. Up on the brae, Wise Janet's cottage had no roof these days. If some tourist thought it *quaint,* the way they do, and bought it for a summer place, he'd find it haunted. She was a Rannoch, Janet, and dirty as a tink. After all my city years I still could tremble at the thought of her. It was just here that Tam McQueen had hit her with a pebble. A wee smooth pebble too—not sharp. The boys did plague her now and then. They were afraid of seeming feart of what they did not understand. I was there that day. Did I not hear her with my own ears as she turned round and ill-wished him? There was real ugliness on her brown, seamed face. We ran away. I was quite friends with her till then; but when Tam died that winter, it was different. He was a great strong boy; you never knew him ill; but he got this blood disease and went before the spring. When the old wife grew bedridden and Father said that I must visit her, I wouldn't go without Nurse. I wouldn't. Miss Lamont said it was just superstition, but she was from the Border.

Another bend; we angled differently. I could now see the last reach of the Shael and the stone bridge. My own Shael breaking free from its dark bonds to empty in the sea. How bright it was! Fresh water from the hills, salt water from the oceans, mixing and closing finally. There was an old tale that this mating bred the first salmon in the far-off days, and certainly they loved the Shael.

Long before I ever held a rod myself, I'd watch them struggling up against the stream—proud, strong, and beautiful. I cried when my first one was landed. It felt like murdering a friend, but Angus said that it was necessary and the fish would know and respect a new Rannoch, so I went wild with joy and ran to Father, but he just laughed.

"That's fine, Aillie, and now it will not be so long, I'm thinking, before you fish for men. You'd best remember that the rules are the same, except that men are easier to play and far more difficult to land."

Old Angus cackled. He thought Father a great wit. But I tossed my head. If you'd offered me a fairy prince, I'd have thrown him straight back in the water. I was content with what I had, a silvery prize.

I could see the glen well now, a huddle of dark trees, though my eyes were rather blurred. There was the tall west tower of the castle thrusting out, and the highest of

the chimneys. That very big one went down straight into
the hall. I climbed it once to rescue a kitten. Ginger . . .
that's right; one of Libby's. He was stuck in a sort of
room a few feet up—quite dark and with a most peculiar
smell. They said a man had lived there in the Troubles.
He must have been uncomfortable.

I was black like a sweep when I came down. You
should have heard Nurse—felt her too! She scrubbed me
in the bath till I was scarlet, and then anointed me from
head to foot with sheep fat.

"Will ye be still, Aillie! I've heard soot burns into the
skin and ruins it."

"You're ruining me already, Nurse!" I wailed.

"And causes cancer," she went on implacably. "Do you
wish to be like yon old Lady Dousie? The puir soul, they
say the pain is terrible."

"I can't help that," I said defiantly. "I had to get down
Ginger, black books or no. He was scared, Nurse; he
really was. There's rats up there, great big ones. Did I not
hear them squeak and scuttle?"

"Ach, the creatures! I will speak to Angus McDhui
right away. We'll all be catching the bubonic plague for
sure! The Black Death, they call it."

Nurse always took a gloomy view, and she really was
afraid of rats and mice. It wasn't only just the hygiene
aspect. She would stand up to Father, drunk or sober; she
stuck to me when any douce town nanny would have
fled; but let her see a baby field mouse, and she'd go into
hysterics.

Poor Nurse! Had young Aillie ever shown her gratitude? Or even felt it in a conscious form? Years too late I
paid her tribute. She'd taken on a child who'd never

known a mother, a half-tamed cub who bit and scratched with insecurity. What hope of success with Father to undo her moral teachings and her earnest training? I was as bad as Ginger in the chimney.

She had one ally, Miss Lamont, and often she'd go down to Holly Bank to pour out her woes. Sometimes this had effect, as on the day when Miss Lamont donned her town suit and snow-white gloves and walked up to the castle.

They shooed me out of the book room, but I just slipped into an adjoining cupboard where I knew fine I'd hear all they said. I had no conscience about eavesdropping and couldn't hope to hear good of myself.

"I'm fond of Aillie, as you know. She has the makings of a first-class person. She's gifted and intelligent. She could go far."

"She'll go too far one day," said Father grimly.

"Dougal, I'm sure she spoke the truth about those lambs, and anyway a riding crop in front of the whole village is no answer. However, that's not why I'm here. I repeat, the girl is promising."

"She's a wee limb of Satan!"

"And aren't you proud of it! You encourage her, Glenshael. She's a cheap form of entertainment when you're bored at home. That wretched Mrs. Wilson does her best but in the face of almost constant sabotage."

"My dear Flora." Father put on his Sunday English drawl. It always boded ill. "You must realize we have somewhat different standards. Aillie is a Rannoch of Glenshael and therefore no rice-pudding miss. You must expect panache from highland families."

"The other daughters of your cateran breeds are quiet

enough. Panache! Dougal, the girl is barely civilized. We
all think it's disgraceful. It must be stopped."

"Are you nagging me, Flora?"

"I'm telling you your duty. Dougal, that child needs
schooling."

"She goes down to the dominie every day. He says she's
quick."

"She needs to be for she's only there one day in three,
from all he tells me."

"Is that so? Playing truant, is she? She'll have another
skelping."

"Spare your rod. It's more serious than that. She wants
enlightened discipline, plenty of normal occupation. Her
mind's like blotting paper, but it soaks up only one small
field of knowledge. Glenshael and district. The child's
starved."

"And you would have her a bluestocking?"

"What a wonderfully outmoded expression! You
needn't be afraid that she'll be academic. Her lust for life
is far too great. It's far more likely she will be a beauty
like her mother, and just as harum-scarum. Where will it
lead her? Into the heather with the blacksmith's son?
Already she has no restraint, no counterbalance of a well-
tuned mind. It's frightening."

"All right. You know so much. What do you suggest?"
Father did sound a little shaken at this point. Men who
are very free in their own lives are most particular about
their daughters' morals.

"A friend of mine has just become headmistress of my
old school in England. I'm sure she would take Aillie and
handle her with sympathy. It's exceedingly expensive
nowadays, but you could spare yourself an annual Rolls

Royce, or two months in London, and use the money better. And incidentally, while I'm on the subject, isn't it time you paid some local bills? There'll soon be real ill-feeling. You can overplay the privileged laird, Dougal Rannoch. I wonder that great pride of yours allows you to batten on your social inferiors."

"You go too far!"

"I shall go much further to protect a child I'm fond of. Unless Aillie goes to boarding school next term, I'll take drastic action on an official basis. I'm serious, Glenshael. And having said so, I shall go."

She won. Beneath her gentleness she was like tempered steel. I pondered on the conversation long afterward. Even before I went to school I was better mannered, less wild, for Nurse said the authorities would send me to some Borstal, which I knew would never do for a Rannoch of Glenshael.

I couldn't have been vain, for all that talk of beauty didn't register. No one agreed with Miss Lamont, not even me. It wasn't till I met Joe that I remembered.

"You could be breathtaking, and I shall see you are. Give me one year, and I'll prove it in six months."

He did. It cost a lot of money. It's only skin-deep beauty, after all.

The bus pulled up outside Holly Bank. There were proper stops with notices, but no one ever used them. You said where you were going and they dropped you at the door, a habit which, after London Transport, I found most endearing. In this part of Glenshael village, a row of solid, old-world villas faced the sea, giving the impression of a formal promenade, though a mere rough of sandy turf merged with the shore.

The pair of trees which gave the house its name had grown potbellied; banks of azaleas still flanked the sloping lawn. They'd never liked the salt much, but they'd survived against all odds. It all looked much the same. True, the front door had turned an acid yellow, and the knocker I had given Miss Lamont had gone. Still, it was Holly Bank and not too unfamiliar. . . . But how strange!

A slatternly young woman in drooping flowered rayon answered the bell. Her coarse red hair and flaccid mouth suggested the hill people, who from time immemorial had bred like rabbits. They were all related to each other, those folk; you simply daren't ask who was whose. Luckily fate had compensated this poor specimen. She had a lovely voice; I listened avidly. It was the speech of home.

"You will be Miss Rayner? Himself was not expecting you so early, I am thinking. Do not trouble with your luggage. I myself will see to that."

"Thank you," I murmured automatically. Good heavens! What had they done? African masks, like some cheap coffee bar; a hideous rug in oily midden colours. No Persian runners, jewel-like on the parquet; no card tray for the callers. The once pastel walls now imitated zebras. I could be glad that Miss Lamont was in her grave.

The narrow hall was introduction to worse horrors, and how I took it all to heart! I'd have been less surprised to find ten years of cobwebs swathing the drawing room like dust sheets, where beneath their prisoning the china dogs, the rose brocade, the Bechstein boudoir grand remained inviolate, above time. Instead I saw lime-green and orange covers vibrating like a humming top. More midden rugs—well, they were quiet at least. By why a terra-cotta ceiling with those curtains?

The impact was so shocking it distracted me. I blinked and forgot to greet my new employer.

Beside his stage décor he seemed almost restful, despite his transatlantic shirt and espadrilles. Considering it was early in the year, he must have found his plunging neckline chilly, but it did reveal a fine crop of hair to offset the thinning at his temples. He was about middle height, a little overweight, and had an indoor look. His eyes, half screened by heavy spectacles, were sharp and observing. He combed me up and down with satisfaction. I'd hit exactly the right note.

"My dear Miss Rayner!" His voice was strong and consciously pitched, as though to quell the Lower Fourth. "What brings you here to Holly Bank at this ungodly hour? Don't tell me that you spent the night in Stranach."

"I'm afraid so," I admitted.

"Ridiculous! The most abortive chime from that vile instrument, the telephone, would have sent me posting, quite incontinent, to meet you. And yet you use the omnibus, that crapulous contraption of the foul fiend. You will agree, perhaps, it's only suitable for rural stomachs. Can I offer you some hyoscine hydrobromide?"

A bicoloured python rock snake! Isn't that how they always talk? Miss Lamont had read the story in this very room, with me enraptured on the beadwork stool.

"I enjoyed the ride," I said truthfully. "There was certainly no need to bother you."

"I won't upbraid you further. We must start in harmony. No doubt you had a very tedious journey which

impaired your judgment. And how is London? Does it
still exist, I sometimes ask myself? My dear Miss Rayner,
do sit down and rest your aching bones." He offered me a
Gauloise, which I refused quite firmly. The room was
already blue with smoke.

"It was a very pleasant journey," I continued. "The
scenery, from Glasgow onwards, is quite splendid."

"Landseer stuff!" he snorted. "So tritely obvious. You
need a special sort of mind to like Scotland—preferably a
century out of date."

"Which describes me exactly, I'm afraid."

"Pray don't apologize. It is expected from my secre-
taries. They all come here to spend a few immortal hours
in faëry lands forlorn. Very forlorn, my dear Miss Rayner. It's a savage life we lead among the oiks and yokels,
and we lack compensations. You will drown on nature
rambles; you will see the mountains once a week, the sun
maybe never. The bread is always stale, the milk
skimmed. The coffee's worse than British Railways' offer-
ings. Which reminds me that you need refreshment. We
shall ring for Donaldina and introduce you to the trials
ahead. She brews a singularly rancid mixture, but let us
not repine."

He was perfectly correct. Scotland is seldom coffee-
minded, but this beat anything I'd ever tasted. I felt a
mild surprise that James Bywater could swallow his so
calmly. From now on I'd drink tea.

My employer talked and talked—in yards, I decided.
Now and again he'd snip off a length, so I'd slip in a
sentence just for luck. He was obviously hungry for an
audience—I knew the feeling. Meanwhile his spate of
words allowed me to adjust to this new Holly Bank.

I was extricated, later on, by Donaldina, who took me
to the former maid's room—a happy choice. It was neu-
tral ground. I doubt if I'd ever seen it in the old days, and
it was very simply furnished from the auction room. The
window looked across the Great Meadow. I could see
exactly where I'd jumped my first pony. A fine herd of
Ayrshires stood knee-deep in lush grass. How did they
make it grow like that? No wonder they said Mr. Forres
was efficient. And then I laughed. Angus would sniff for
sure at such a troop of portly, lowland matrons.

The forest to the left, the first windbreak of Douglas
firs to the extreme right. Enough but not too much. The
actual glen was safely out of sight. I would live in an
annex with a feeling of detachment. Here I could grow
acclimatized and take things slowly.

I was pleased on the whole. James Bywater was in my
range. I'd met his type often. By evening I was fairly
settled, resigned to everything but Donaldina's cooking.
I'm not a chef myself but beside her I was *cordon bleu.*
True, I could blame indigestion if I grew depressed.
Meanwhile I wondered if James Bywater's despairing
prose was influenced by tortured gastric juices. One look
at the potatoes sent me slimming, though from my former
sex-symbol standards I was skinny as a broomstick.

"Have some more greens?" said James Bywater. I
should have called them *browns.* I wrapped up what I
had in pickled onion and refused more reluctantly. The
fact was country air gave me an appetite, a thing I hadn't
had for years. It seemed a shame to chew stuff like
pemmican and dream of Yorkshire pudding.

"I hope you're not dismayed," continued my employer,
"now you have glimpsed your future drudgery. The work

is not inordinate, however. Your leisure you will find the
greater problem. I do not love method; it doesn't suit my
kind of madness. I tend to work in spasms, part-time one
day and double-time the next."

"I'll fit. You'll see," I reassured him. "And as for
leisure, I'll know what to do with it. In London, when my
work was over, travelling, shopping, housework ate up
every spare moment. I'm looking forward to the saner life
very much indeed."

"Easy to say, but you forget you are no longer in the
Great Wen. Its disadvantages are paid with dissipations.
In a week from now you will begin to mention that
society as you understand it is nonexistent in Glenshael.
The weekly film was *vieux jeu* in your infancy. I fear I
eschew television as a moral principle. If you wish to
offset my style by reading twelve-and-sixpenny romantic
novels, a van calls once a month, weather permitting,
which means such things are rare as Dead Sea scrolls."

"There seems quite a population here. . . ."

"The peasantry? Our Donaldina is an average specimen. I hope you have not much in common with her.
Their sports, you know, are whist and breeding, the
wrong side of the blanket preferably. They spawn assidu-
ously. Were there a prize at some Olympic level for sheer
fruitfulness, Glenshael would win it. As for the men, they
poach and drink as well."

"But there are several larger houses and some bunga-
lows."

"Ah, you refer to the petit bourgeoisie. I'm afraid, my
dear Miss Rayner, we cannot escape them, even here.
Such worthy people, but so uninspiring. For instance,

there's a Scott-addicted bank manager retired. He's read *The Antiquary* thirty times."

That would be Mr. Bain, whose wife sucked peppermints.

"Also retired, a linen draper who thinks the devil has an English accent. Not to speak of a tax gatherer, a small mean man quite unlike dear St. Matthew. He's by far the worst. His hobby is to climb hills and social scales. They all have wives with ill-fitting dentures who mingle with our maiden ladies, diggers for mud to throw on whited sepulchers. It seems a pity there is no collective noun to cover village gossips."

"Would *basket* do?" I entered in the game.

"But admirably, my dear Miss Rayner. I shall use it from now on. A basket of bitches by your leave. They will soon approach you, sniffing cautiously, reminding you of your employee status but with curiosity outweighing snobbery. They attribute gross sexual orgies to this household. I sometimes feel quite sorry that I disappoint them. But it does not do to gratify vulgar suspicion and give the undeserving satisfaction."

I reflected that though James Bywater and Miss Lamont had little else in common, it was pleasant to find Holly Bank was still a culture outpost, ruled over by mild arrogance of soul. Its owners had a narrow broad-mindedness. They thanked God they were not as other folk.

"How about gentry to complete the social picture?"

"Ah, yes. We have a Great House, Castle Rannoch. It's up the glen, among the trees. Pure Mrs. Radcliffe. Ivied towers and bats and owls, and no doubt skeletons in every cupboard, rattling like castanets."

"I hear it's haunted."

"It is, my dear Miss Rayner, by a dwarfish, horror-comic figure."

"The chieftain girl?"

"We may disregard mere phantasmagoria. This is a creature called McDhui, otherwise known as Angus. If you value your skin—and don't we all?—never take scenic rambles in the glen. I admit that I am not cast in the heroic mould nor wish to be. Faced with a trigger-happy ghillie, I am not ashamed of flight. When pursued implacably by this blood-lusting character with bullets ricocheting round my head, I am no athlete, but I achieved a sprint. I did not even pause to think of coronaries."

"He *shot* at you!"

"I see you are amazed; I'm not surprised. But this, my dear Miss Rayner, is Glenshael."

"If this Angus person really shot you, didn't you complain?"

"Naturally. When I had recovered from my unwonted exercise I dipped my pen in vitriol, of course. Addressed the local laird, this monster's mentor. It seemed a minimum requirement that he should apologize for near murder on his land."

"He didn't?"

"You don't know our Mr. Forres. He regretted, if you please, that I had been put to inconvenience, but pointed out that I was trespassing and his gamekeeper merely did his duty at a time when poaching was a menace. He understood I'd suffered no material hurt, and remained mine etcetera, A. J. F."

"But that's iniquitous! He sounds a brute."

"A bastard, my dear Miss Rayner; and, what is more, a Scotch bastard. I do not aim to shock you, I merely use the mildest word available. More I could say, but will contain myself. I merely illustrate you go near Castle Rannoch at your peril."

He continued to enlarge his theme, while I sat seething and incredulous. I certainly intended to pay the glen a visit. And if Angus played his daft tricks on me, there would be trouble! And as for Mr. Alastair J. Forres—who the hell did he think he was? Father would have been more courteous to a tourist. Poor James Bywater! I'd soon even for him. Nice little man to treat in such a way!

"My temperament is mild, as a rule." He was still talking. "The landed gentry go their way and I go mine, conscious that I should find no great refreshment absorbing absolute alcohol with old Sir Hector Dousie, or conversing with the supercilious laird of Anacher. Once a year, it is true, I dine with Lord Mantum. In leaner days I contributed to his gutter press. Even then my enjoyment is somewhat mitigated by the wild strains of bagpipes in my ear. I do not understand the ruling classes, but we keep an armed neutrality. Forres, however, invokes stronger feelings. He may pepper me with bullets or run me down with his damned ostentatious car. These are minor insults. What I cannot forgive is his pretension-crushing. We are the only two Cambridge men in this district, contemporaries at that. I once reminded him. He wasn't the least interested."

"How silly! When you're neighbours."

"True, he was up at Trinity while I sojourned near the G.P.O. He was born to the silver spoon, while I subsisted on a shoestring scholarship. He wrapped himself in blue scarves and scored at Twickenham. But though our worlds were different then, we might have made them coincide a little in this desert. He made it plain at our first meeting that he did not agree."

"He sounds a bore. You're well out of it. Anyhow, isn't there a real gulf between such sporting playboys and the true scholar? If I were you, I'd feel very superior."

I'd said the wrong thing altogether with the best of intentions. He fairly glowered at me.

"Considering I was the modest possessor of a two-two in both parts of my tripos and A. J. Forres took a double first, I fail to find basis for superiority, my dear Miss Rayner. The Gods smile on their favourites."

I could see the statement seared the soul of James Bywater, and couldn't think of a constructive reply. My anger against his persecutor grew. I always had been very partisan. The more I heard about Mr. Forres, the less I liked him. My false cousin was right on that score, it now seemed. Fancy a man like that at Castle Rannoch! It made me wild. I found that I was plotting mischief like my long-abandoned Aillie.

An enemy, but I had lost my headquarters. My usual battlefield was not available. One Alastair J. Forres had taken my strategic position.

# 6

## Speed the Plough

I SETTLED DOWN to work. There was no great backlog and the current book went forward in vast jerks, punctuated by meditation pauses. Compared with my last job, I'd found a sinecure. I soon grew quite attached to James Bywater.

He too seemed satisfied. By next evening I had become "dear Alice." We had to keep up London standards and flourish Christian names.

"So you went into the village? How did you get on? A far cry, you'll say, from E.C. 4."

"I caused a stir. It was rather amusing. Consoling to be of some importance in a community again."

"Misleading, my dear Alice. They only wish to know the worst of you. Remember that."

"You can't blame them. Wickedness is exciting. You ought to know. You'd never sell your books if it weren't."

I was happy as a convalescent from a major operation,

carefree, now silly dread had proved unjustified. I had
been terrified, so I thought I'd get the ordeal over and
made a special expedition to the post office.

Old Mother McNichol still lived in her wee cage, her
queer unblinking eyes watching the village savings. As I
went in, an awful silence fell, the chatter of the starlings
stopped abruptly. Jean, who presided over groceries and
suchlike, had turned as old as her reptilian mother. I
gulped but still advanced. They melted back and listened.

"Five-shilling book of stamps," I said hoarsely. "Isn't
it a lovely afternoon?"

"It is indeed," Mother McNichol hissed. "You've
brought the good weather with you, I am thinking."

"Yes, it makes me wish I were on holiday."

"You are not? Then you must be Mr. Bywater's new
lady, come for the typewriting. Ach, that will be a comfort to him."

"I hope so." I gave a jolly outsize grin, feeling for all
the world like Joyce Grenfell. "This is a really glorious
place; such scenery. There must be splendid walks."

"I would not say it was so grand at all, Glenshael. I
have heard there are many better places for the scenery
further south. There's not so much to do here, you know.
You will be missing all the English ways."

"I'm a tremendously keen bird watcher," I said. "I saw
a Manx shearwater this morning."

Real tourist talk for an admiring audience. But here
there could be no half measures. Two feet away stood
Annie Gair turned matron. I reckoned I could still beat
her at hopscotch. Goodness! She must be nearing twelve
stone.

Yet afterwards I felt a little sad. It was too easy.

Next afternoon, James had a fit of meditation and typists were not welcome. I had no plans, but certainly a walk might clear my head. It was almost second nature to make for the Great Meadow, though I kept firmly to the left towards the forest ride. There began my first real climb since I left hospital, nearly a year ago. They'd thought, for a long time, I'd never walk again. To me it seemed utterly improbable; I never could accept it. Of course I would! I'd show them! . . . And I did.

With pine needles soft beneath my feet, assurance grew. I sniffed the resin on the air and listened to the gossip trees. Soon I was stalking like a cat, circling around my confines restlessly. There was new planting further up, young feathery larch.

Out of the dappled wood, on to the open hill, where I put up a grouse and heard her chicks near by. Beneath me lay the Sound, green as glass. A large ship plowed along in the far distance, the fishing boats were busy nearer shore. The hills to the northwest were dark violet; Stac Liath wore lilac-gray; behind me massed Beinn Dubh, the black hill. . . .

I stood for a long time, gazing there. Everywhere were skylarks, singing from heaven or near it. I envied them their lack of inhibition. It was a moment for thanksgiving, but I found myself stiff-kneed and mute. Humans are very poor at self-expression, and their lack of spontaneity is sad.

All of Glenshael! I blessed it unawares, and like the old man in the story my burden fell away. There was new circulation, the long numbness loosened, and the dead soul I had grown used to began to take its leave.

It was rebirth, yet at first no pangs at all. I roused myself, a bairn again, and just as irresponsible. I went along the ridge much faster, with all my cares forgotten, till at the slope downhill, I had an urge to run, and a silly mess I made of it through lack of practice. But never mind, I was not dreich Miss Rayner any more but a young creature back in my own place.

The path reached the lower cairn which marked the entrance to the glen. A blue hare started up and stared at me most disapprovingly before he loped away. From where I stood, I could see Castle Rannoch plainly—the new house and the old towers knit together. It was a history book in stone, written up till now by my own people. Pure Mrs. Radcliffe? Well, maybe. We'd always been a bit Gothick.

It beckoned me. Nor did I hesitate to answer. Who was this Mr. Forres anyway? I'd suit myself. Since I'd walked miles out of my way, this was now my shortest route back to my tea. As for old Angus, when had he ever found me in the glen unless I wished it? Did Aillie Rannoch rattle twigs and stones? Ach, and I'd lay a bet that I could take a salmon right under their noses. And I might. You'd hardly call it the black fishing. They were Rannoch creatures.

I moved cautiously toward the water, tensed with anticipation. The Shael, my Shael, my own river! It danced to see me there. It *knew* me; someone knew me! Up till then it seemed I had been in the mountain with the Good People, returning to great isolation from my kind.

I crouched beside it. Stiff-kneed no more. I washed my face, quite ceremoniously, in the icy stream. If I had been reborn, I needed neo-baptism.

The river laughed and chattered in its friendly way. Yes, I'd been disappointed at my own success. Unreasonable. I'd taken so much trouble, all the time wanting . . . what?

It used to be more difficult to fool people. Then I'd be sneaking down the glen, as I was now, the Shael hiding my quiet tread with all its noise. I'd run through the shrubbery, slip through the side door, but just when I felt safest Father would have me by the hair.

"Come here, you wee devil, and tell me where you have been. Your nurse has been asking for you these four hours. Ach, you're in rags, and scratched from head to foot. And that's a nasty bruise you have forbye."

"I fell, Father."

"Did you now? But where? Have you been up at the old quarry, Aillie Rannoch?"

"Ach, no, Father. I know fine the quarry's out of bounds. I walked toward Beinn Dubh, Glenshael. Only I lost my footing and fell into some brambles."

"Beinn Dubh, is it? Aye, the eagles' nest. You'll break that neck of yours before you're reared. Were you after the eggs?"

"There were no eggs, Father. The young ones are hatched out already."

The trouble was about Father, he'd been brought up just like me, so he knew all I'd be doing which I shouldn't. Stretches of Rannochs lay behind me, all skelped for the same mischief. The hard thing was to sin originally.

"So you were at the nest and fell down?"

"I did not! I climbed on by the Lum. It's quicker, after all."

"Aillie, do you not realize that real mountaineers come to climb the corries of Beinn Dubh, with ropes and fancy gear to make it safe? There's a seven-hundred-foot drop behind you, and the rock is treacherous. Experienced climbers have been killed, Aillie, doing no more than you did today. I see you came home by the bog."

"It's shorter."

"I'd be a happier man if you sometimes were afraid of something. Don't fidget when I speak. Listen, for once. I'm not going to beat you this time, though your grandfather gave me six for the same thing. But if I find you at the nest again, without McDhui or a grownup, I'll double it. Use your head now and then. Away with you, and mind—apologize to Mrs. Wilson properly. And for God's sake, wash your face before she sees you!"

You never knew which way he'd swing, Father. When you were all keyed up for a skelping, he'd just smile. Or he'd be laughing almost, and suddenly he'd change. Nurse punished me, of course—but that was different. She'd say why, she'd say when, and then would get it over. But Father, no! Sometimes he'd shrug me off with something near congratulation; next he'd let fly at almost nothing— nothing at least that you could understand. I never cried, however bad it was, till I was on my own. There was a dreadful fear inside he might greet too, and this was all instead of tears.

I never knew what like of man he was. I doubt if he was happy—ever. And he wasn't always fair to a wee girl, letting me carry half the weight of things which troubled him.

But ach, he was my father, and I never loved a man so well!

Now I threaded down the byways of the glen. The trees closed in, the paths grew moss-grown and springy. The Shael had dropped below me now but still I could watch it. It played a sort of fugue, chasing itself in sound, as it flirted in the sunlight and rested in the shade. The great deformed oak bent double still to see its image in the stream. The Deer Rock hadn't toppled after all but still remained precarious at the watersmeet. Shael Glen. I had been born and bred beside it. One day I'd die but hear its music still.

Unfortunately people, unlike rivers, seek for words, and the clumsier the better. Psychological trauma, for example; that was a fine term for a simple thing. You went on living like the twisted oak, successfully enough, but no one really touched you. You forgot how to give. In the course of time you grew used to it. Without your traumas and your complexes, you might be nothing, empty as that poor child on the train going back to school. Ten years of unreality I'd had.

Well, I'd proved myself. I had whatever made a true Rannoch. I didn't need the tribal setting, the prefabricated lot. Without a single prop, I'd fought my way to triumph. A hollow sort of destiny, as things turned out, but I had made the grade. That was the essential difference between me and Father, who had sunk without his good name. I couldn't. Once challenged, I must win.

I hadn't failed my blood, but Father had. I ought to have been with him. I'd have stopped him surely? Even

at sixteen, I knew myself the stronger. Why had I been at
school? He must have needed me—needed me dreadfully
—I was all he had. And no one left for me.

"Angus. I feel strange. Have you a dram handy?"

"You're ower young, wee mistress."

"For this, yes. Ach, thank you! That's the flask Father
gave you. He was a fine man, Glenshael."

"Aye, he was that."

"I'll not forgive myself, Angus. He must have wanted
me. I left him all alone."

"Come away, Aillie. You have seen enough. Will I put
the sheet back now?"

"His winding sheet? No, leave it. I wish to look a little
longer, so I'll remember what they did to him. His own
people, Angus—folk he loved and trusted. He had more
use for his pride than most, and they shamed him. I'll not
forget."

"Your fine aunt from Edinburgh talks of a quiet
burial."

"We'll not have that. Is he not Rannoch of Glenshael?
Let them all come. Every man and woman of them. I'll
see they don't forget either."

It was scarcely worth the trouble—cowards that they
were. Pale, frightened faces staring at me. Years later I
could see I cursed myself, not them. Well, maybe that's
the way it always is.

While they shuffled home in whispering groups, I went
alone to sit beside the Shael. I chose the last pool of the
upper glen, a lonely, lovely place. Goodbye—and yet I
left myself in its keeping. She still waited there, that

frightened girl. They were all waiting for my return, not
to Glenshael but to what I'd left behind.

Now I knew that I must turn this last corner, however
great my reluctance. This was why I'd come. I had to.

The path, to my surprise, grew artificial. Neat flag-
stones brought me round the final rock. I stopped
abruptly. What had happened? The trees hacked back,
my grotto living desert. Of all the hideous atrocities!

Where were the smooth, flat rocks? The white gravel?
Why all this sluggard water? I could not bear to look as
the truth closed on me. They'd dammed my Shael!

My river dammed, and damn the man who did it! How
dare he? And for God's sake *why?* And what about the
salmon?

It had been my favourite playground when I was
young. A secret place with a fine rushing stream. Now it
was all clogged and muddy, full of wee sickly water
plants. I followed the new path down to the edge. The
barren rocks were dotted with rare Alpine plants, each
with a little stick beside it with the name in Latin. It was
a miniature graveyard.

I never saw a place changed so, and for the worse. I had
returned to a bairn's burying ground. It was too sad for
me altogether. For the first time in ten years, tears rolled
down my cheeks and I not caring. The poor Latin plants
were wanting home, as I had done. You could see that
they were wearying for better days. They longed for
crocodiles and chamoix and such beasts, the snow-capped
peak, the steaming jungle. Strange what you pass
through dry-eyed and what you cry for, but the sadness is
the same, and the easing.

I slumped down at the water's edge and sobbed on, the way I hadn't dared after the funeral. Then it had mattered far too much. You must be sure of clambering back to sanity. They had dammed my Shael, but I had broken clear; and now, were there enough tears in the world for ailing plants and lost folk, and the dreams which had died with them?

Poor ruined Shael! Poor alien flowers! Poor Aillie Rannoch! No place to stay, no firm spot on which to stand. What would I do, now I had found her once again?

# 7

## This Is No My Ain Hoose

"ARE YOU BY any chance aware that you're on private property?"

The cool, haughty question seemed momentarily irrelevant. I took no notice.

"Or to put it bluntly, you are trespassing on my land."

I looked up then, gathering my straggling wits. Good Lord! Sourpuss turned Forres!

I was the more furious because I had no handkerchief. Bad enough being caught like that when you're a child; grown up, it's quite intolerable. Though at that moment I was not wholly certain which I was.

He stood above me on the bank, leaning against a shooting stick. I wondered, horrified, how long he had been there. To think I had admired his nose; he knew how to sneer down it. Confounded, supercilious interloper! He needn't speak like that to me!

"You must be the atrocious Mr. Forres," I said. "I understand trespassers are more likely to be shot than prosecuted. You've forgotten your gun. How careless!"

"These are my grounds."

"So you have said before. You're welcome to them. Perhaps you think I'm poaching, but I would not bother. There'd be no more than goldfish in this dreich pond, I'm thinking. Swimming among those silly, homesick weeds. Are there not water lilies enough upon the moorlochs? And they fine, strong, and beautiful in their own place?"

"*Nuphar lutea* or *Nymphaeaalba?*" he enquired almost courteously.

"I neither know nor care. They're local plants; indigenous, not sad exotics. Would you say those half-dead things were worth the barring of the way to the spawning grounds themselves? The path of the salmon? You have destroyed the work of centuries—and all for nothing."

"Yet what I make of my own property is my own business."

"I think not! Someone must tell you what you're doing. The salmon have their ways; the young fish remember home. And you dispossess them. We speak of *Salmo salar,* Mr. Forres, since you're so fond of Latin."

"And since you're sentimentally obsessed by salmon, allow me to relieve your mind. Had you trespassed just a little further, you'd have seen a diversion and a fish ladder."

"Fish ladder! Would they be liking such a thing? It's not the same at all."

"It's adequate," he said.

No words can describe my turmoil of emotion. I was erupting into a mad volcanic rage. Confronted by the usurper himself, it took all my control to keep my hands off him. Was it not bad enough that he had bought my birthright like a block of shares, without this wanton desecration of all I held dear?

The difficulty was, I had to raise my head and look up when I spoke to him. Look up! To him indeed! It made me wild. He was closer now and far too tall. He had unfair advantage.

"Did I not see you on the train?" I changed my angle of refraction. "I thought then you looked antisocial. I'm evidently a shrewd observer."

"As you please." His eyes were coldly mocking. "I admit I would rather not have the policies of Castle Rannoch strewn with abusive tourists."

"But I'm no tourist, Mr. Forres. I work here for another trespasser, a further victim of your incivility. Mr. Bywater. You don't know him, do you? Or don't want to. As for me, my name is Rayner, Miss Rayner, in case you wish to write to me, remaining mine, etcetera."

He raised at least two eyebrows.

"Odd irony! So you'd like me to write to you, Miss Rayner?"

"I would *not!* I'd tear the letter into pieces. I'll tell you this, that young man on the train was right. Do you by any chance remember how he summed you up? Ach, but you don't know any better, do you? A southron parvenu, quite ignorant of highland custom and hospitality. You don't know how to treat the common people. Did he not say so to his pretty Sassenach?"

My adversary frowned. It seemed I'd made a touch and high time too. I was now safely beyond the stage of warding off tears. I clawed verbally.

"That young whelp!" he murmured.

"Glenshael himself. The castle's future owner. I look forward to the day, Mr. Forres. He has ingratiating manners."

"You might take lessons from him."

"And so might you. You set the tone. I agree: some people are no loss—to anyone."

"I am afraid that you are right, Miss Rayner, though it is a terrible way for a lady to be talking surely? Have I not one foot in the grave already, and you would have the other join it? I am surprised indeed that you could speak so to an old and ailing man."

I reeled at this backhander and must have looked as silly as I felt. I hadn't even realized that I'd been talking highland until that mocking lilt reminded me. He did it well, with just enough exaggeration. As there was nothing obvious to say, I preferred to whistle back my scattered wits.

"Yon poor dreich flowers are all I have to comfort my declining years, mistress. Would you be grudging me such simple pleasures? I am afraid I am a thought discourteous to trespassers, but it's the nearest I can get to sport these days. A douce woman would have pity on a vulgar upstart. Ach, as you feel so deeply for the salmon, can you not feel for me?"

His crow's-feet, wretched things, had deepened; his eyes had narrowed till they danced. The mouth relaxed and twitched slightly. Then he really smiled.

I never saw a smile like that before. It lit him up, and pulled me like a moth toward a lamp. There was a long silence, just the water and the soft brushing of the trees. Better like that. Better for what?

"I must go," I said absurdly.

"Nonsense. After all this we need some tea. Belated highland hospitality, Miss Rayner. You must encourage such a decent impulse surely?"

"I shall not! Nor will I disturb your hermit life again. I have trespassed upon your grounds and on your time, Mr. Forres. Good afternoon."

"I'll see you to the gate. You might be intercepted further."

"I'll take that risk; and if I'm shot, I'm shot. Perhaps in such circumstances you would be good enough to call the doctor or the undertaker, whichever's indicated."

He laughed outright, appallingly infectiously.

"It's a high horse," he said. "Be careful not to fall off."

"You are most considerate—belatedly," I snapped.

He needn't laugh at me. He'd spoilt my glen, he'd damned my Shael, he'd ordered me off my own soil. He wasn't fit to stand in Father's shoes . . . well, no one was. He was too tall and big and confident. And worst of all, he'd seen me howling like an infant. I'd not forgive that in a hurry. I hated him!

I set off at a sharp pace, avoiding policies and house alike. I'd had more than enough for one day, that was sure. Yet I felt better now I had an enemy, a ruthless adversary, tricky as they come. A bastard, yes; a high-land bastard too. Beyond that southern drawl, I knew my own. Not much to choose between us in a straight fight. But dare I take him on? And why the hell?

The lower glen; I'd done the wisest thing. It was easy to forget the smile of Mr. Forres while the mainstream of a shrunken Shael limped towards the waiting sea. Did he

think, our persecutor, he could tame me too? Well, he
could not—and needn't try.

Before I reached the bridge, I paused and gave thought
for the first time to my appearance. A small rock pool was
not an ideal looking glass, but it showed me quite enough.
Tame me? Where had my thoughts been wandering?
What man would wish to anyway? I never saw a worse
mess. My awful wig was wild; my eyes all red and
swollen; I looked like a tink. Miss Rayner was bad
enough without a sort of spae-wife superimposed. And
there was mud all down my dress from that damned
pond.

Thank heaven that he was antisocial. One hoped he
wouldn't dine out on my behaviour. He owed me nothing.
I'd given him no cause for chivalry. It wasn't just that I'd
been rude, I had been Aillie Rannoch. Anyone might
have overheard. I'd not last long that way. Instead of all
this talk of fighting, I must hold my tongue and keep the
peace.

Miss Lamont always said I should learn to curb my
temper, but I'd forgotten that I had one.

I felt safer in Holly Bank. I always had. When I was
little and home troubles piled up unbearably, I'd slip
through the windbreaks and run across the Great
Meadow. And Miss Lamont would sit me by the fire and
tell me stories.

In those days I didn't have to type them.

I worked that evening. James burst with creation. It
was difficult to keep alert, I felt so sleepy.

Miss Lamont would not have found his stories *nice*.
She was not exactly prudish but she had set standards.

"You'll hear a lot of talk about what nowadays they call sex but I call self-indulgence, which is one of the two deadly sins, my child; the other is stupidity."

"I thought that there were seven, Miss Lamont."

"The traditional set are merely categories, Aillie. Invented probably by men, who have poor visions but a fondness for preaching. Love is a many-splendoured thing, so don't confuse it with adultery. What people grasp inanely is generally wrong."

James Bywater droned on. He had some pretty turns of phrase, though sometimes these clogged up the narrative. I don't mind preaching about something, but to use words to fill a pit is like setting a trap. Then too, his characters annoyed me. I was glad they weren't my parts. His women had no entity. They were particularly ingenuous, designed exclusively to go to bed with men and like it.

"Where were we?" James enquired after a long aside about industrial scenery.

"We were on the bomb site with a girl with tight jeans and neuroses. Why was it still a bomb site anyway?"

"Did I say she wore a black sweater?"

"No, she has nothing on except her jeans, and they'll have to be off at any moment. Now I come to think of it, no wonder that she has neuroses. Life would be so much easier if she had a sofa and a peignoir."

"My dear Alice!"

"And a boudoir," I added sleepily.

"I think it's time we had some more dialogue."

I tapped away, my mind on strong black coffee.

When the telephone bell rang, I rushed to answer it, relieved to be away from Gauloises for five minutes. Of

course, I never dreamed that it would be for me. Why
should I?

"Miss Rayner? I do apologize for bothering you so late.
Alastair Forres here."

"No bother," I said guardedly.

"It's a long chance, I know. But maybe you could help.
We were talking earlier on about the railway journey."

"I was," I agreed drily.

"You remember the girl? The fourth member of the
party? You mentioned her, I think." As I made no reply,
he tried again. "I didn't listen in till I myself came under
discussion, so I probably missed the main point. Did she
by any chance introduce herself? I'd like to know her
name."

"Diana Marston. London. Shop assistant."

"But that's not right, I'm sure."

"It's what she called herself, and what she registered as
at Stranach. She ought to know, you'd think."

"I wonder." He sounded very thoughtful. "I'm sure it's
wrong. It's damned irritating. I can't remember who she
is, or where I've seen her, but I know her certainly."

"Yet she does not know you. . . ."

"Yes, that may be a clue. I'll work on it again. No
doubt it will come in due course. It's been hovering round
my mind ever since I saw her. Was that young man a
pickup or by prearrangement?"

"Since when was I omniscient? Spontaneous, I'd say,
on her side at least. I wouldn't know about Mr. Rannoch
—a more devious type altogether."

"I'd guess his name was really Smith or something.

This seems to be a masquerade of sorts. Well, thank you, Miss Rayner. . . . Is that *your* name by the way? Or have you the same trouble?"

It was extraordinary, the trick he had of throwing me off-balance. Of all the things to say to me! How fortunate he couldn't see my face—and nor could I!

"Just call me Alice," I said swiftly. "Through the looking glass, of course. Now do you want me any more? I'm working!"

"At this time of night? You ought to go on strike."

"I have to earn my keep, you know. Not being a tourist like your friend Diana."

"That 'D' is right—and the 'M' too. . . . I've got her! . . . Triumph . . . Thank you very much."

"Well, who is she? After all that fuss."

"No matter. I'd not like to spoil her fun. Not much of a life really. She probably deserves a bit of privacy."

"So although I helped you, you won't play?"

"I think not. Though I am grateful. I can now sleep in peace."

Exasperating man! As if I cared about his night's rest! There wasn't much for me.

My mind was out of gear. I tossed about in bed unable to digest piled-up experience. Even Diana Marston failed to moor me. Who was she anyway? Why had he changed his tune so quickly? All along I'd felt uneasy about that wretched girl, and it was still simpler to concentrate on her. Did Cousin Rannoch recognize her too, and if so why the interest? She needed privacy . . . "not much of a life really." And Mr. Forres didn't want to spoil her fun. But was *fun* compatible with Peter Rannoch? I knew the cut of men on the make.

I would try to visit Stranach, and take another look at the liaison. It would keep my mind off other things to see the direction of Diana's way. And a slight remove from Glenshael and its problems would surely prove cathartic.

# 8

## Strip the Willow

NEXT DAY I put my resolution into practice. It was apparently the habit of staff at Holly Bank to call Saturday a half-day and spend it in Stranach.

"And no doubt you will stay for the cinematograph performance," said James Bywater. "It is the weekly dissipation of the natives. Remember to take several handkerchiefs. The alternatives are laugh-till-you-cry comedy or very treacly tragedy. As I have an inborn inability to judge which is which, I keep away and spare myself a lynching."

"May I leave it open? See how I feel?"

"By all means do. Supper is cold and movable at the week-end. And take the back-door key."

It was not till I reached Stranach and had completed some necessary shopping that I bothered to check on the film or interest myself in entertainment. And then I gasped. The star was Anna Rayner, another entity of

mine I had thought safely dismissed. Heavens! I should
have changed my name completely. Half measures never
served. But was there danger in this odd coincidence?
Surely any comparison between the actress and the typist
was pretty odious. The film was old, as James had
prophesied. I was nineteen in those days—which, come to
think of it, was not so far removed from Aillie Rannoch.
Thank goodness Joe had polished me extraordinarily before he launched me on my meteoric course. My *image*
certainly did not suggest a schoolgirl. At the time, I'd had
no qualms.

Joe had found me playing small parts in repertory,
eking out a bare living as I worked and learnt. He
groomed me, steered me, perhaps projected dreams
through me, and with him, for a time, I achieved quality
and thought it was my own.

But idols are the sum of their worshippers and topple
easily. You wouldn't find an Anna Rayner film in London
now. You had to go to Stranach, of all places.

No film, then. I never liked to see myself on the screen.
Gael that I was, I found it not quite canny to inspect my
external self. Moreover, one species of nostalgia at a time
was enough. The problem was to keep below saturation
point.

I made my way to the hotel in search of Diana and tea.
Unfortunately there was no sign of either of the young
people, and I ate scones in gloom. It seemed the lesser of
two evils to look back on my lost career and even to
accept that ill-paid drudgery stretched interminably
through the future. The trouble was I'd tasted different
kinds of power and now regretted all of them. Still, not
much point in wondering if both abdications had been

mistaken, when it was far too late to mend. The best thing I could do was return to James and kill this new mood with hard work. Stand, wait, and serve. It was the average lot and excellent discipline for me. I'd played the grasshopper, and much good it had done me, so why not try the ant?

"May I clear the table?" a young waitress was asking.

"Please do. I'm leaving anyway. I have to catch the Glenshael bus."

"Ach, mistress, perhaps you didn't know. It does not go till after eleven on a Saturday. It waits, you see, until the film is over and everybody ready."

"But surely . . . ? How ridiculous!" She'd be right, of course. There weren't so many buses after all. How could I have guessed this would be the one alteration in the timetable? The only alternative was walking home.

Walking! Odd I should think that automatically. A month before I'd have dismissed the idea as impossible. Had I really been fighting fit for some time and never noticed, because in London the mere struggle for existence had mopped up all reserves of energy? With health, as well I knew, the drabbest picture could seem brighter.

To allow the waitress opportunity to clear, I transferred into the bar, and my better mood was soon rewarded by Peter and Diana joining me. Not that Diana's face exactly cheered me up. The de'il tak' the Fause Rannoch! She glowed with achievement; her eyes were sparkling; she'd found some Grail and saw Sir Lancelot. Stupid child! Fancy mistaking him for a gentle knight. A slippery customer, for sure, smooth and cold as a serpent in Eden. I noticed he was far more wary, making a mental note of me this time, as though I cropped up far too often. Well, it might teach him caution.

From snatches of their conversation, I understood they spent most of their days together and her walks had turned to driving in a car he'd hired—a development which I mistrusted. I would have liked to learn much more, but they stayed for only one drink and departed to high tea. It seemed that they were going to the film, so they were safely stowed.

The exodus was general. The bartender produced a paperback. Most visitors took advantage of the weekly orgy, and it was still too early for the regulars. Someone had left *The Scotsman* on my table. I began to do the crossword.

"One down is *sycophants*," a voice interrupted. It was information which I needed, though not from this source.

"Good evening, Mr. Forres," I said coldly.

"May I join you? We seem to be the only people here."

"As it's a public place, not private grounds, I can't prevent you. But I am just about to leave."

"No truce? I'm disappointed. You were almost civil on the telephone."

"Then you interrupted a boring stretch of work."

Despite my lack of welcome, he sat down, so I stood up pointedly.

"I've missed my bus," I said. "And I really must set out for home before it grows too dark."

"You don't intend to *walk?* It's miles of hard going."

"But health-giving exercise, Mr. Forres. And there's a short cut by the cliffs, I'm told."

"Which is quite tricky in broad daylight. You'll either break your neck or sprain your ankle, according to the hour. Anyway, my car's outside. What's wrong with that?"

"I don't accept favours from you, Mr. Forres," I said candidly.

"But this is neighbourliness—a virtue you yourself advocate strongly. However, it's absurd to argue. I'll run you back, of course. Finish your drink and have another."

"I'd rather walk," I countered ungraciously.

"I can't imagine why. You'll just punish yourself, not me. And anyhow, don't you think perhaps both of us should do slight penance for our behaviour yesterday?"

His wretched smile was lurking with its curious inclusiveness. I'm not surprised. We sounded silly; me in particular. I remembered there was safety in convention and disciplined myself.

"It's very kind of you," I said belatedly.

He laughed. "You see you can if you try. And now, Miss Rayner, was that medium or dry? We'll drink to the armistice."

My protest, though not effective, was quite genuine. To mix alcohol with the owner of Castle Rannoch was, I felt, unwise. This was as ill-advised as driving on a busy route with judgment impaired. But what was the alternative?

"I find you a most irritating man," I said. "You go your way and everyone must follow. Your call last night, for instance, was in questionable taste, and to make matters worse, you ring off having made me crudely curious. This meeting, however, does allow me to pursue the question of this girl. Why won't you tell me who she is? And are you here to introduce yourself to her?"

"Certainly not. It would remind her of what she must wish to forget. I've only met her once and that was at a

funeral. Her whole family were killed at one fell swoop—
a plane crash."

"Poor child. Yes, that explains it. You might remember
her while she took note of no one. I'm sorry that she
really is an orphan, and wish she chose her company more
carefully. That Rannoch man is no fit companion for a
young girl on her own. But he's hanging round her all the
time, and she's completely taken in by him."

"Surely not? Anyone with any sense at all . . ."

"She doesn't come into that category. She's a romantic
in search of a dream which may well prove a nightmare."

"You take it all to heart, Miss Rayner. And probably
exaggerate. That bogus clan-talk is of course a bore but
relatively harmless. Moreover, she is very young—still
looks like a schoolgirl, which is why I recognized her, I
suppose; that and an uncommon flair for spotting faces."

"You may have forgotten," I protested, "that the im-
mature do have feelings, and very sensitive they are.
That child's in danger, if only of making a fool of herself,
which can be damaging at her stage of development and
leave an ugly scar."

To shake him up, I added an outline of my findings, for
if he had some contact with her background I thought it
as well that he should know. I was glad to see him frown.

"He could be a reporter," he said when I finished.

"Why in heaven's name? In what way is she news? But
for my money he's not."

"If your guesses are right, she'll hardly tell him who
she is, which is some safeguard."

"Need you be so mysterious? I've given you my ver-
sion, now it's your turn. Besides, I don't trust male
judgment in matters of this kind."

"Very well"—he shrugged—"as we're no longer on an open line. Have you ever heard of Deborah Mansfield?"

"Do you mean the Richest Girl in Western Europe? Of course! I read my gossip columns. Are you absolutely sure of that?"

"I'm certain."

"Yes, I see now. Unfortunately it all ties in. She's run away to find someone who'll love her for herself—a Marks and Spencer's Cinderella. And what she turns up is Prince Charming Rannoch, of all unlucky things! He'll know who she is, right enough. No doubts on that score. I'd guess he worked it all out beforehand, saw her safely on her train and caught her up in Glasgow with the late interception putting her off guard. She played into his hands. Scotland's a fine country for a fortune hunter, with its useful laws concerning minors. A marriage settlement's a better game than blackmail. The wedding ring will be his first object. I've been on the wrong track. Her virtue can't be threatened till she's hooked."

I was so upturned, I'd melted into monologue, forgetting that I spoke aloud. I was surprised now at an interruption.

"I shouldn't worry. Her trustees will soon fix him."

"I wonder. They'll be in London, I suppose. That's a far cry from here. Young Peter's on the spot and doing very nicely. I wonder how the money is arranged. They often get their millions upon marriage. I remember now that there were brothers in that crash. No one would think to tie her up securely when she never was expected to get the lot."

"They were half-brothers," he corrected with a yawn. "The girl has been bred in divorce circles and with that amount of money will herself, no doubt, have several undersirable husbands, if not more. The cousin who looks after her is honeymooning with her fifth at this moment. I read it in the paper."

"She sounds most unsuitable," I said.

"I face facts. Heiressess are fair game and soon adjust to the inevitable"

"What a callous point of view! Here is a decent girl who has as much right to a good and useful life as someone poorer. Why should she be victimized because she's rich? Something must be done."

"I see you have a natural bent for saving brands from burning. But what can you do? Call in the police?"

"I wish I could. But no. A state of outraged, misunderstood rebellion would play into his hands. A close friend or a relative might intervene; but even so, extreme tact would be needed. One false step and he'd run to earth and take her with him. At least they're in the open now, and he playing safe. I don't see he can actually seduce her when he's so far from the money. What do you think?"

The gray Forres eyes mocked me with maddening amusement.

"I don't pretend authority on such matters," he said.

"No, of course, you're a woman hater. I'd forgotten. But it isn't funny, Mr. Forres, so you needn't be so superior. Any normal person would be troubled to see a girl infatuated with that snake. And I'll tell you this, that Castle Rannoch talk had some foundation. He wants her money to secure a background which will feed his vanity. He's set his heart on being Rannoch of Glenshael, so look out for yourself."

"Rather than *die*," he said, "I'll sell—at a substantial profit."

Hostility returned. You'd have thought the place was half a dozen eggs, the way he talked about it. I had forgotten this was an irresponsible usurper, was none too pleased to be reminded of it.

"No doubt that's all you think of—money! You're not in London where no one cares a damn. I'm not ashamed of my intrusiveness. I wish I could do more. But what?"

"I'll tell you this," he mimicked softly, "you'd argue the hind leg off a donkey. Haven't we had enough of Deborah Mansfield for one day? There *are* other subjects of conversation."

"What, for example, when I hardly know you?"

"What we do next perhaps. Do we dine here? Or would a change of atmosphere wean you from your pet obsession?"

"If you think that I stay here for the pleasure of your company, you are mistaken. I'm passing the time just, till you're ready to go home."

"That settles that," he answered with a smile, "so let's be on our way."

The Forres Jaguar, which I now saw for the first time, was somewhat ostentatious. It was very like the car which had killed Joe and smashed up my career. I sincerely hoped I would not have to clench my teeth or wipe my palms. I was always glad long, low-slung vehicles so seldom came my way these days. One does not like to be a nervous wreck, governed by coward reflexes.

I breathed more freely when I found he drove leisurely, nosing round blind corners, hugging the grass verge. It allowed me to reflect that it was not unpleasant to touch the world of luxury once again, though I had often thought my ups and downs occurred to eradicate Rannoch extravagance and grandeur.

There was no conversation then that I remember. We preferred silence. It was not until we reached the pass that it was broken.

"Just look at that sunset!" said my chauffeur. "The western sea has infinite variety, but this is more than usually histrionic. Shall we pull up to the cliff edge and have a front-row seat in the dress circle?"

He did not wait for an answer. And this sunset was weird. I'd never seen its like before. The Sound was a rainbow lake with its silhouetted islands shimmering till they pranced like imps with all hellfire behind them. You had to watch in case the devil himself rose up out of the sea with his pitchfork. Was that why I felt vaguely apprehensive? It was like an old doom picture right enough.

Nature is economical. It knows when to leave you with a taste for more. The pageant faded with great subtlety, and dusk was there.

"I'm sure the meeting house at Stranach doesn't run to quite such gorgeous Technicolour," I said to pass the time when it was over.

"Yes, I'm glad I didn't go to the film. I meant to."

"But I had no idea. You should have told me. I'm sorry, but you did insist on offering me transport."

"Never heed. I prefer the substance to the shadow."

"The sunset? Yes, it was very fine."

"I wasn't referring to the sunset. And anyhow I have seen all your films before. And most of your appearances on television."

I was so disconcerted I couldn't speak at all.

"I told you I'd an eye for faces," he continued with a smile. "Deborah's, it's true, eluded me for some days; yours was far easier to place."

"It's impossible!" I managed, still half-gasping. "For no one recognizes me. No one!"

"Then I must be the rule's exception, Miss Anna Rayner. Remember that your name tallies, and that you did treat me to a free dramatic dress rehearsal in the glen."

"That wasn't acting, Mr. Forres. Nothing like it. This is absurd—it's witchcraft. Do you know people who used to work with me, day in, day out, now cut me in the street? Yet you, a complete stranger, pin me down like this. It's not as though I even met you in my stage days. I remember people too, and your manner would stand out, if nothing else."

"We once dined in the same room—at the Savoy, I think, but no reason you should have noticed me. My dear girl, don't look so worried and alarmed. We needn't talk about it if you'd rather not. I merely thought it would be honest to put the cards down on the table. I'm sorry if it fusses you. Forget it!"

"A lot of hope of that!"

"Poor Anna! Was I somewhat clumsy?"

"Don't call me poor—or Anna. My name is Alice, and it's best that no one should know otherwise. The trouble that I've taken with my new start! Cards, is it? You've knocked my card house down. What have you passed on? Have you told anyone?"

"Not even Craigie, as it happens. He's away to Fort John on a visit."

"And you won't? Please, Alastair."

He raised his eyebrows slightly at my pleading. "Of course not, if that's how you feel. Now for heaven's sake relax and trust my tact a little. Let's talk of cabbages and kings, if that's what you'd prefer."

His smile was curious, no longer challenging; a twist of the mouth, a softening of the eyes. And then to my surprise, he took my hand, imprisoning it, and looked amused at my sharp reaction. I did not like the way which things were going and preferred to misinterpret them.

"I'll thank no one for pity, Mr. Forres."

"Who's offering it? And who is Mr. Forres? It's no time at all since I was *Alastair*. We'll keep it that way, if you please. Part of my blackmail terms."

"Alastair," I corrected with demureness. I rather liked the name.

"That's better. And this isn't vast compassion. You're oversensitive—look how you ruffled at the touch. I'll tell *you* something for a change. In the train I labelled you douce town mouse; in the glen, a fighting cat; but I see you're nothing but a prickly hedgehog after all."

At which he lifted up my hand and brushed it against his lips to lay it comfortably on his cheek. His bones were a good shape, his skin provocative, the roughness lurking in the smooth. I swallowed hard, and half my pride with it.

"I'm sorry, Alastair," I said meekly.

"I bet you are! Why, you nearly smiled just then! I didn't think you could. You always look so cross."

"I do not! Anyhow, what is there to smile about? Apart from all the rest, I've landed in your power, and now I'll have to be polite and well conducted."

"I'm looking forward to it very much—and to the smile."

He made me wild. But I was thinking and gave him a grand royalty flash meanwhile. I couldn't afford *not* to wheedle, so I'd best turn on some charm.

"I'm still shattered, Alastair," I went on most apologetically. "I can't imagine how you guessed. Please tell me everything. There might be some point I must rectify. I'd gone to so much bother to look different, and I didn't think I was a bad actress."

"You're a very good one, to my mind. But I think you have perhaps been too professional. Surely what you have done is to retailor an old part in which you grew old ungracefully? Wasn't it a play? About four years ago in the West End? At any rate, it came to mind the first time that I studied you. I thought it rather funny. Clothes, hair, and even mannerisms were all of a piece. Complete reduplication."

"Oh, Lord!" I said unhappily, as I realized what I'd done. It was true. I'd put on the old wig, and all the rest came back. I was surprised he'd seen the play. It didn't have a long run.

"I expect I'm the only one in these parts who attended." He seemed to read my thoughts in his maddening fashion. "They like something a little brighter when they do go to town. And if you'd take my advice, keep off the Ibsenesque. It isn't you."

This I ignored. "Allowing all you say, it might not have been me."

"No, but it was amusing. Frankly it didn't actually occur to me that any entertainer this side of a hundred

would choose to look like that with any possible alternative. And certainly not one like Anna Rayner, whom one
connects with elegance and charm. It was only afterwards
I remembered that no one had heard of you since your
accident, and I wondered if you could have cut adrift,
swinging too far the other way in some bid for self-
protection. It would depend upon the quality of vanity,
among other things."

Again the dig. I let it pass. "How did you know for
sure?" I asked persistently.

"Yesterday decided me. I ceased to doubt. I'm afraid,
you know, you forgot all your lines. It was very good but
the wrong part, and besides you lost all your ageing
dignity and made me feel my full thirty-nine years. I'll
say no more, my interesting hedgehog, or you'll prickle."

"It's still fantastic, Alastair. You know it is."

"Perhaps I have sixth and seventh senses—shall we
leave it so? And instead you'll tell me, Alice through the
looking glass, exactly why you try to represent a maiden
aunt."

"Have you ever read a Bywater advertisement? He
likes them auntish."

"Why work for that ass anyway?"

"He's not an ass. I like him very much. And the job
suits me fine. I couldn't stand that city office any longer,
and the break never seemed clean enough in London.
Always I stumbled up against reminders. So I came
here—miles from anywhere or anyone. It all added up."

"But what about your career? It's ridiculous to throw
away such talent so thoroughly. You gave a lot of pleasure to a lot of people. Did you never feel it was a duty to

go on? Allowing for the knock, the readjustment would have been far easier if you'd gone back into harness as soon as you'd recovered."

"Are you lecturing me, Alastair? It's damned easy to talk. What is recovery? When I came out of hospital, I looked awful and felt worse. It was obvious I was finished. My face, my figure, and my energy were my chief stock in trade. Acting needs stamina. You give and give that pleasure till you drain away. It just can't be done without marginal reserves. Besides, I'd reached the top of my species of tree. I'd rather be remembered as I was. Nor was it only illness. I had lost my Svengali. Joe took so little credit at the time, but the only part I ever really played was Trilby. My sort of vanity is not to be caught out, and live in a fool's paradise."

"And Joe was the producer-lover killed in the same crash?"

"He was."

"And you were just about to marry him, the papers said, and start another film."

"Which was scrapped."

"Your reaction's natural but misleading. At first you would feel powerless without him, price of lost love perhaps. But equally it could wear off and you might want the chance of standing on your own, unless your heart was broken finally."

I stared unseeingly at Stac Liath. The dusk was deepening into immense privacy. What a strange background for talk of Joe, who belonged to grill rooms, country clubs, and plush hotels! No, I had not loved Joe past all repair. He was fun, he was a good friend and a great

artist. Marriage? Well, it had seemed to fit in at the time.
Ambition takes some curious turns and is useful for
warding off cold feet. Joe and I lived in the same world
and had the same professional integrity. Moreover, we
enjoyed each other's company.

"All that 'good friend' stuff happened to be true," I
said aloud. I might have been speaking to the twilight
and the hills. "We never really got around to high romance or bedroom farce. I was very fond of Joe; I
respected him enormously, and I was absolutely mad
about his work. The funny thing was, when he was
removed I was glad of an excuse to stop the game. It
wasn't only that I didn't want to slide downhill. It
seemed a chance to be someone that I liked better. I was
sick and tired of being just a puppet, however cleverly my
strings were pulled. And as for love and all such grand
emotions, puppets don't experience them. They're made
of wood."

"Poor Pinocchio!"

"It's true. I wish it weren't. For it's not exactly canny
being someone else. And yet the habit forms, and life's a
bag of tricks. Emotions are for sublimation only. In their
raw state they'd soon be stumbling blocks. When I believed I had a real vocation, the ruthlessness was necessary and worthwhile. But disillusion teaches wisdom—a
bit too late."

"How very elegiac!"

"Goodness knows why I'm talking in this way. I've
never bared my soul before. The shame is when you get
started, immediately you overdo it. To sum up—acting's
out."

"Then you must learn to stop," he said, and moved his

arm around my shoulder. I wondered if I should protest, but it felt warm and right.

"How do you know so much about me, Alastair? You sound like a fan magazine."

"I never noticed that you lacked publicity, and in point of fact, at the time of your crash, I was in hospital myself, for the umpteenth time, and bored as hell. I made a cult of reading all your press to pass the endless days. I'd enjoyed your acting, so I felt a special sympathy. I nearly laughed yesterday when you suggested that I write to you. I did once; I managed a whole page before I tore it up. It was really too intrusive, on soberer reflection. A retired life breeds strange enthusiasms. I found you an apt contrast to James Boswell."

"So I should hope! But I thought you were a woman hater."

"I expect I used you for a sex substitute," he replied equably, "which is, surely, what you set out to be."

"Alastair Forres!" This time I really laughed, which made me relax more against him. "You know, I'll pay you back for that when I am ready. I expect it's just the women who hate you, and I am not surprised. Meanwhile, it's nearly dark. I think that we should move. I'm tired of staring at the Sound."

"You could look at me. . . ."

"Why should I? I can hardly see you anyway. And I do think we ought to go. Someone might notice us parked here."

"How dreadful! Does it matter?"

"To me it does. The last thing I wish to do in my position is to attract attention, especially while that film is in the district. My object is to be most dull and respectable. I must be above suspicion, Mr. Forres. And from all one hears, you yourself don't dally; at least not openly—so I can't see why you need begin with me."

"Your reputation in my hands." He laughed softly. "All right, stickly-prickly, we will be circumspect."

"In a place like Glenshael," I continued sturdily, "we can't even be that, not that I want to anyhow."

"I wonder," he replied.

It was my cue to look at him defiantly, but the half-light shadowed those too clear-cut features and softened his uncompromising contrasts. He was bonnie, Alastair, like that. It came to me, I'd never seen a face I liked so well. His black brows hitched a little mockingly and yet his eyes were serious. My heart beat very fast.

So there it was. I couldn't speak for my uneven breathing. I was worse than Deborah Mansfield with far less excuse. It would be difficult to find a man more inappropriate for this old game. But all power of choice had been removed. I wondered if he'd now kiss me, and it was possible that he was wondering too. What would I do? What say? It would be interesting if he did. Just once, once only, for one minute. At least it would disperse this impossible suspense, this speaking silence.

I was practically sure that it was going to happen when he removed his arm abruptly and started up the engine. I'm afraid that I felt very disappointed, which was disgraceful—when I hardly knew him. It's not as though I was addicted to that sort of thing. I should have been relieved.

Yet I could have gazed at him all night. My shoulders felt quite cold without that arm. His profile wasn't quite the same. It held too much detachment. Of all the stupid things! I'd fallen headlong for Mr. Alastair J. Forres, the last man in the world for me to tolerate. James was quite right, he was a bastard—and probably an amorous bastard too!

All of which shows it's possible to love your enemy, which at least is a religious thing to do.

# 9

## The Bonnie
## Breist Knot

WHEN THE CAR had finished bumping back onto the road, I found myself absorbed in fancies. They set my wits awry, so that I only surfaced when I saw a hare caught dazzled in the headlamps beside a five-barred gate.

"You've taken the hill road," I protested.

"Only just noticed? I generally do, which is why the gate is left open. Stand by now for the cattle grid; it makes an awful racket."

"But this leads to Castle Rannoch only. I wanted to be dropped off at the crossroads. It really is too bad. I haven't even got a torch."

"And yet you talked of walking home! And what's your hurry? We haven't yet had dinner."

"Nor will we—if you mean together. It's quite out of the question."

"Still thinking of your reputation? I told you I would guard it, and by taking this route we dodge the village gossips altogether. You can ostensibly return by the late bus, and meanwhile we'll be quite on our own in the castle."

This had occurred to me as well, if the Craigie person were away and the other staff nonresident. Two was misleading company for one in my condition.

"We can raid the fridge," he continued cheerfully. "It's always full enough to feed a zoo. Besides, you ought to see the house, having thoroughly explored the grounds."

Maybe he thought himself funny. I did not. I was reminded merely of the previous day and the truth that I was not yet calm enough to face new shocks. The fact was that I dreaded going home. I wasn't ready. Would I ever be? It seemed a special sort of masochism.

"You appear to assume that I enjoy your conversation." I quelled my lurking fear by lashing back at him. "I'm glad you do remember yesterday. So do I. You were outrageous."

"So were you. We equalized."

"You started it. You know you did. *Are you aware . . . ? to put it bluntly . . . !* I reacted naturally. People don't speak to me like that."

"I thought not. You reacted as I hoped you would. Shock tactics. A gamble but it worked. It seemed a bit premature to offer you my shoulder and my handkerchief."

"You made me furious on purpose?"

"More or less. It cheered you up considerably."

"I've never heard the like! You think that anything becomes you, Alastair. Look at you now, assuming I shall spend the evening with you and eat your salt. Why, you might be anything, for all I know. I won't do it."

"Would it help if I promised faithfully not to rape you, or even murder you unless you drive me to it? I'm offering you a meal only. Let's not exaggerate."

"I'm not hungry."

"Then let us hope we stimulate each other's appetites," he said ambiguously. "It's too late to argue; we're nearly there."

This reminder silenced me effectively. My panic grew. It might be just as well to tackle Castle Rannoch. It's wise to get the worst over soon. I could then retreat without feeling I had dodged the issue. With past and present stuck in limbo, I had to fight through to the active future.

It was dark when we reached the main drive; no moon to hang like a lantern and guide me home. That's when it's bonnie, Castle Rannoch, a mysterious silhouette of possibility. By day it's not so much at all. You wouldn't put it in a glossy magazine. The new house had been built at a bad time, apparently to please Prince Albert. However, by some happy chance or necessary thrift, they'd used the same old stone from our quarry and it gave a certain harmony and mellowed well. If you weren't too dreadfully aesthetic, you didn't wince, but it was too pretentious for Miss Lamont. As for me, I thought it dignified and proper. The vast porch, now caught in the car headlights, had medieval elaborations past belief.

It was strange to enter that way. Nurse always made me use the other doors. But I was now a caller and grown up. A guest of Mr. Forres. Me!

"Come in!" He frowned at my hesitation and took my

hand to lead me through. I clutched it like an eager child. It steadied me. It was his house. It would give me clues to him. I should be interested. I was in love with him. A sedative for more important aches was necessary and I must swallow it.

"Let me take your coat." He did so. Despite my resolutions, I could not speak. My mouth was dry, my throat ached abominably. It was even worse than I expected. The hall had scarcely changed at all.

I was left on my own. Our big furniture appeared to have become a fitment, even the awful antler chandelier. Suppose there was a ginger kitten up the chimney . . . ? The carpet was different but still red. Not much that you can do with highland houses. You need the stags' heads, the stuffed fish. They're always very fond of antique weapons. The duelling pistols were all paired. When I had left, there was one missing—the sheriff's deputy had it. It was a fine, chased Manton—valuable. Well, better that it went to strangers.

"Sorry to be so long." I, of course, hadn't noticed. I stood there in a sort of trance—of horror.

"Good Lord! Your teeth are chattering. I didn't think it was so cold. You'd better come in to the fire at once."

Still silent, I went reluctantly into the book room. Here, at least, was translation. Miss Lamont always said the room had possibilities, and now I saw precisely what she meant. The wood-block floor was harvest gold, the rugs were glowing meadows. Alastair's books were mostly new editions and fitted neatly into long low shelves. The air was swimmy with efficient central heating, despite the huge log fire. Colour and comfort, taste that was impeccable, and a very lived-in room.

I said so in the interests of politeness.

"Understandably," said Alastair. "It was my prison for a long time, so naturally I made the most of it."

Instead of pondering on this remark, my attention roved toward the furniture, in particular a china cabinet. It was unusual in design and had three Prince of Wales feathers.

"Where did you find that?" I enquired abruptly.

"I bought it second-hand in Stranach."

"It ought to have a set of china dogs," I murmured. "Derby and Rockingham, with wee baskets and cushions." It had been my favourite piece of furniture at Holly Bank and looked all wrong full of Venetian glass, however pretty.

"You have conventional taste," he said.

Well, so had Miss Lamont.

I settled down upon the sofa and told myself I was imprisoned too. Nurse might be waiting in the schoolroom, grumbling about the tear in my best skirt. As for upstairs, the first door on the right . . . I wouldn't think of it. His face was covered now. For in the end they did take him away. He couldn't be there still. They were only watchers . . . listeners. I *would* not think of them. It was safe here.

"Are you sure you feel all right? You're shivering again and look as though you'd seen a ghost."

"Perfectly, Alastair." My voice at least was firm. "Though they say this place is haunted. Don't ghosts trouble you?"

"Not other people's."

"What of the glen by moonlight?"

He laughed. "You refer, no doubt, to Aillie Rannoch.

She doesn't bother me and I don't interfere with her. You could say that we had a working partnership. Poor child! She's better than wire fencing for keeping off marauders. Even poachers here are seldom local men. They respect her far too much and give the Shael a wide berth."

"Perhaps there are no fish to catch," I said pointedly.

"There are enough, and she's as good as three Mc-Dhuis, as the old man well knows. It's he who perpetuates her myth. It halves his work and both of us enjoy our privacy. People don't stroll in after dark, I find. We're taboo."

"Are you really as unsociable as they say?"

"I'm self-sufficient. In an overnarrow groove perhaps, but that's the way I like it. I've got out of the habit of suffering fools gladly. Yes, I am all they say."

"You carry it too far. I was horrified to hear that James Bywater was nearly shot."

He laughed again, this time whole-heartedly, and I noted that a lot of years rolled off him so he looked just like a wicked schoolboy. "Poor Bywater! I was hoping that he'd sue me. He ought to have been grateful to McDhui; he needs to lose a stone or two of weight. Not that anything went very near him. He just didn't like the bang. How you can stand him I don't know. Pompous, affected windbag!"

"He's as good as you are any day. He's kind and clever and no fool. I admit he has a rather heavy manner, but it does no harm to anyone. And even if you don't care for him—need you be rude? I'll tell you this, a rich father and a double first should make you more polite, not less so."

"I love annoying you. You say the most extraordinary things."

"I'm glad I entertain you."

"You and McDhui both. And don't blame me for Angus, who is Bywater's real persecutor. The sacred glen is his department. I inherited him from the Rannoch family, whom he serves fanatically, alive or dead. My function is to pay him and to ease him out of scrapes. In return he allows me to live here, if I behave myself."

"It's your job to discipline him. He's your responsibility."

"You tell him so! Mind you, he isn't wholly mad. We have had gangs up here after the salmon. It upset Angus very much. For the rest, I'm sorry for the old man. His world collapsed too late for him, and now he only has his glen left. I don't know if you've heard his history, but his ghost stories are his revenge upon the village. He's too fond of his Aillie to allow she might be dead, but alive they'd all have easy consciences."

I'd grown used to myself as a subject of discussion, so I went on with my private inventory. Another souvenir of Miss Lamont was the same size of piano.

"Do you play?" I asked Alastair, to try and change the subject.

"You sound afternoon-tea. The correct answer is, of course, 'a little.' I have also read several good books lately and saw two plays when I was last in town."

"You make conventional conversation difficult," I said.

"We started wrong. No point in going back, in view of our extraordinary progress."

And as if to illustrate our intimacy, he transferred to the sofa and placed his arm back in the old position. I raised my eyebrows haughtily, but he only laughed.

"That feels much better, and you know it does."

He was right. The ghosts receded, and my tension

ebbed away. The more so when his second arm went round me. I made no form of protest, even settled nearer, and then sighed contentedly.

As I remember, I was less conscious of the man than the happiness he gave to me. I could block out all other complications, a new numbing process. At that moment it was very welcome.

"Alastair." I articulated his name slowly, just for the pleasure of its sound.

"What, love?" he murmured absently, as though he thought of very different matters.

"Nothing. But your motives interest me. You're being kind to me, I think. Not that I mind. I'm not prickling. Only Miss Alice Rayner seems an unappetizing dish. I suppose it's all that talk about the glamourous Anna. You assume I've grown conditioned to full sex-symbolic treatment and must miss it. In other words, a mild spot of *tendresse* is therapeutic."

"You flatter me. I've never claimed to be an altruist. I just feel slightly daft, that's all—and want you that way too. Let's be alive and warm and close and damn the rest. There's time enough for reasons."

"But Alastair . . ."

He clapped a hand against my mouth and smiled into my eyes. "Swim with the current, love. Don't analyze the sea. Let's be absurd and like it. Life's meant to be enjoyed on such rare occasions as there is opportunity."

Sourpuss. It was still there, his shrugged-off mistrust, but I didn't really want to know its cause. To maneuver attraction, you must stick to the externals. And my own inmost problems were enough.

Meanwhile he cupped my chin and watched me quizzically. He had doll's eyelashes, as black as night. Swim with the tide? What happened if you drowned? The current, even at this frivolous level, demanded a strong swimmer. I'd always thought I was.

"You raise such fascinating problems, Alice Rayner. I've never felt a burning need to scalp a girl before. Won't you remove your hair, now you are warmer? I think it might improve you—make you a thought more *appetizing.*"

"Don't you dare!" I said, but he tweaked it just the same. My own hair was very short like a wee boy's and most unfashionably curly.

A queer delight came into his eyes; I caught it.

"Why, you're a nut-brown maid," he said. "And how I like you!"

I'm not sure how it happened, but my cheek was on his cheek and I found my fingers stroking down the magpie wings. His heart was thudding worse than mine. I felt it through his jacket. I'd been groping for this moment all my life, and the miracle had happened.

I can't remember the first kiss. It was a sort of faint with your eyes open. Everything blank, all thought suspended; even sensation kept at bay, a wild beast poised for the attack.

But timelessness is not eternal, logic or no. I came to, knowing I was facing something new to me, beyond all outposts of imagination. It need not be the same for Alastair. Who knew what he was feeling? I was responsible for my behaviour without much instruction. Before I'd always called the tune, but this was different.

I was feeling very solemn and important, when Alastair

began to laugh. He flicked my nose, and kissed each eye, and went on ruffling my hair.

"What is so funny?" I asked, hurt.

"You, my magician—you, my stickly-prickly. Why, I've even made you *look* like a wee hedgehog with your dainty pointed face and stick-up hair."

"Well, you're a badger with those fancy streaks! What is this? *Woodland Friends?*"

"Could be. I'm feeling juvenile. You slice a generation off my age. You make hungry where you most satisfy. And God knows what else you do to me."

"I'm hungry too," I said. "Quite literally. Did you ask me to dinner?"

It was a side-step, but it might be to the point. It was possible this floating feeling was starvation. I never could think straight on an empty stomach. Leave that to real mystics.

The kitchen was a revelation. Impossible to recall old Morag's gloomy torture chamber. What wasn't automation was formica, and very bright and comfortable too. I'd best admit that faced with Craigie's idea of a supper, awful greed overtook me. Alastair raised his demon eyebrows, piled food upon my plate, and then sat back to marvel at me with something near to admiration.

"Ought I, as local squire, to visit Holly Bank with baskets of provisions from the Great House?"

"Wolf to Red Riding Hood? It wouldn't be a bad idea. For I live on pemmican. I really do. In London, when I could eat anything at any time, I didn't bother; yet here I think of food subconsciously for hours on end. I even grill myself imaginary steaks in bed at night. It's maddening."

"Have one now."

"No thank you. Just some more ham and that drum-stick, if it's going."

"Another roll and butter?"

"If you insist. If I lived here, I'd grow enormous."

"You could stand a bit more weight. I wonder if I need a secretary."

"I'm sure you don't. You'd be too familiar, if not actually vulgar. There's more in life than food."

Strange how one chopped and changed with Alastair. One minute I was all racing pulses, the next we laughed and everything was right. It didn't matter what we said or what we talked about. I'd been deprived of domesticity for years and the ease he conjured up was wonderful, more satisfying than more sensual pleasures. I smiled at him across the table, as if I'd always seen him there, offering an embarrassment of riches to a pauper.

Back in the book room, we ended up with real coffee. This time we automatically sat side by side with me curled up against him.

"Alastair, I'm wondering why you live here. You're not a highland rhapsodist; you're no sportsman. And goodness knows you have no need of space for entertainment."

"All places were alike to me when I bought Castle Rannoch. I suppose you might say a mausoleum in a garden of Persephone was appropriate—appealed to the vestigial traces of my sense of humour. Glenshael understands disastrous things. It's seen enough of them." He stirred his coffee thoughtfully.

"But that's morbid!"

"Of course it is. And very apt. For I came here to die."

"Alastair!"

"Does that shock you? Well, you did ask. Those are the facts, and Glenshael was the answer. I felt in need of ghostly company. The atmosphere was right. Hardly worth pulling down the blinds if I reached the coffin naturally; and if I hurried up the process with a bullet, I wouldn't be the first."

I suppose he felt the rigor that ran through me, for he held me rather closer. "Now I have shocked you. That's just what I mean. If you learn to live with death, you cease to be a suitable companion. They never mention that in fiction when the doctors give the hero a year to live, though they mean a year to die in."

"They did so to you?"

"Well, not specifically. Medicine is not a particularly exact science. Things were so hopeless I volunteered to be a guinea pig; the useful solution. As your friend Rannoch pointed out, I'm no loss to anyone—might as well gamble on a kill or cure. I thus, quite inadvertently, became a wonder boy of the wonder drug—and here I am, still cooped in Castle Rannoch, not living exactly, but existing."

"I see. At least I think I do. You are better?"

"I'm cured, they say. It isn't quite the same thing. The wonder drug was worse than the disease and crazily depressive. One pulls back slowly, learns to live again, but why one hardly knows."

"Ach, Alastair, that's no way to talk. But I've felt exactly as you feel, and it wears off. I bet you made a greater effort when you were really ill. I did. And it's a shame to end with hypochondria."

"Don't look so anxious. I'll recover. The reorientation

takes time and enthusiasm. Though I see our parallels myself, I had a longer dose than you. Ten years of slow disintegration, and all's to build again. I need a stimulus."

"Yes, something to occupy your mind. I was luckier because I had to earn my living straight away. It was hard at first, but it did keep me going. I hadn't time to brood. There were times when I was young when I hadn't got a roof above my head, nor the price of my next meal in my pocket. You don't let that happen twice, if you can possibly avoid it."

"I run this estate myself."

"Better than nothing; but you're not a farmer, are you?"

"No, I'm a mineralogist."

"Then it's high time there were more minerals in your life. You need them badly."

I was glad to hear him laugh again, the gulf safely bridged. "Another brand to be snatched. How you collect them! You're welcome to reform me. I enjoy the process, though in fairness I must say, I do quite a lot of work. The surest sign of my recovery is that I take an interest in the business side. When my father died, there was no need of me, but now I'm stepping in. I have a burst of activity in London, after which I come home to recuperate."

"As when I first met you? You did look tired."

"I usually soft-pedal for a week or two, but you see how I'm improving. That was only Tuesday, and I'm *dallying* already. Moreover, I feel fine. It must be knowing you. What you think, my pretty?"

Beyond the smile he still looked sad, so I put my arms

around him for a change. I wanted to repay all he had
lost. You could see he'd been a great strong boy who'd
taken illness hard, an athlete resenting his inadequacy. It
was necessary to reassure without words, to patch his
vanity and make him whole. It was good to have something to give him, though it made me love him more.

Success of any sort is noteworthy. Somehow, sometime,
the balance changed, and I was all the more enslaved for
being dominated, when I least expected it to happen. I
was not quite sure about this expertise. It seemed a little
glib.

"It's time for more conversation, Alastair."

"Is it? What can I say? Your eyes are like the deep
pools in the glen."

"Poetic and superb! Are they really?"

"The ones a man could drown in. Really, truly. And
they have sunlight in them and are beautiful."

"Goodness! What else?"

"Nothing. I can't look beyond them at the moment.
Nor would I wish to."

I think he meant it, but he made me shy. The first sign
of true love is clumsiness. You have to be a poet in an
ivory tower to do it justice—emotion recollected in tran-
quillity. In life you precipitate what you would most
avoid.

"Alastair, you are very clever. You must devastate
females by the score. How come you have remained a
bachelor? I doubt if it's from want of opportunity."

He dropped me as if I'd scalded him. Then he got up
and leaned against the mantel. I realized I'd said the
wrong thing, but all else was confusion. It was the first
time he had taken silly teasing without good humour, but
now the smile was wiped clean. His eyes were narrowed,

all the wave lengths jammed. Perhaps he thought I had
been angling. Well, I had not. Rather make matters worse
than have him think so.

"And a wife could have been a help," I pointed out.
"At least she would have kept the social pot boiling. It
would be far easier for you now to start again. I think it's
a pity that you didn't have one."

"The devil you do! Do we really need a post-mortem
for each kiss and compliment? Why the hell don't you
leave well enough alone, especially when you asked for
it?"

"How dare you say so? Did I ask for that lift home,
and incidentally never got there? I was against this
evening with you all along, and said so, Alastair, in plain
terms. I'll tell you this, I'm glad you are a bachelor. I
would be very sorry for any girl who married you, so it's
just as well it didn't occur to you to throw yourself
away."

I was furious, and so was he. He didn't even look at me,
but I saw him play his tattoo rather quickly and knew
this was trouble.

Yet when he spoke, his voice was very cold, which gave
him an advantage.

"In fact, I threw myself away, as you call it, as soon as
I came down from Cambridge. So I am not a bachelor at
all, just for the record."

"I see," was all I managed. Damned if I'd apologize.
My security collapsed and my illusions. Yet I was not
surprised exactly. I found I had been waiting for sub-
merged reefs. I wasn't meant for happy endings. I might
have known that love too was a slippery pole.

"My mistake was natural," I added with more poise.
"Nobody seemed to think you had a wife, and 'just for

the record,' Mr. Forres, I don't compromise myself with married men. I have a sort of horror of private eyes, like some folk have for spiders."

"I said that I *had* been married. I doubt if there's a microphone beneath the cushion."

Immediately my thoughts ran to divorce, which after all he had discussed rather callously that very afternoon. But it was clear the bitterness had not dispersed for him, and thrashing round my muddled mind I found an explanation. I suppose I wanted badly to hurt and hate her, for I couldn't stand the thought of Mrs. Forres. Had she left him in the lurch when he was ill? Run off with someone else who was better company? There are women like that. I don't think much of them. Poor Alastair! It made him bleak to talk of her.

"She was undoubtedly the reason," he continued coldly, "that I raised no protest about dying."

"Sounds very grand." I couldn't bite back my impatience any longer. "But it's nonsense to waste the one life you are given. No woman's worth it. Why not forget her and be done?"

"I'd think less of myself if I could forget. We were happy—we were young. She died when I was twenty-five—a long time ago. People forget, of course, and I don't talk about it. I find it very difficult, you see. She was a specially fine person, far too good for me, but quite capable of moulding a husband out of poor material. She was utterly unselfish. . . . She understood integrity. . . . She was also very lovely, to my mind."

I saw her, through a glass darkly—fair and angelic, handy with a harp. No wonder I had clung to bitch divorcées. I could do without another ghost, especially an enshrined paragon with an uncompromising guardian.

"I'm so sorry, Alastair." Nothing more you could say, and anyhow he didn't listen. He had a sort of faraway expression which didn't match his clipped speech.

"We'd known each other all our lives," he said, "which made a deep bond. I don't look back on three brief years. We had much longer. We did everything together from nursery days; we never looked at anybody else. Marriage was automatic—an extension just—the same but infinitely better. We had a house in Chelsea and we both loved London, though we were always planning somewhere in the country for when the family came along. I often wonder if I chose Castle Rannoch because it contradicted all our dreams so flatly. Deborah liked unpretentious, friendly houses with pretty gardens."

"Deborah?"

"Yes, I think that's why I inhibited the Mansfield girl. I do try to avoid reminders, as a rule. No point to them."

"I oughtn't to have made you talk. It was clumsy. You've said enough, Alastair. I understand."

"Might as well finish, now I've started, and get this matter clear. I was going to say, we were both rather ambitious. As only children, we wanted a large family while we were young and could enjoy them. I think six was the target. God! The arrogance of youth! When she started the first baby, we were both delighted, but we took it all for granted. How was I to know? She'd never had a serious illness in her life, and she held the modern view that maternity is stimulating, healthy—to be taken in your stride. Right till the last moment, she was well—looked well. When they told me they were both dead, I had to see them before I could believe it. She looked surprised—that's what I couldn't bear—surprised. And I knew why. I ought to have been there, despite their regulations. I failed her for the first and last time."

"And you blamed yourself for that?"

"I felt like a murderer. I'd given her the child. She trusted me. The baby was born alive, had nothing wrong with her, they said, but she seemed to have no interest in living. I expect she was too small. And what with one thing and another, I went under. The whole business knocked me sideways. Both my in-laws and my parents offered me a home, but I preferred to live on in the Chelsea cottage with all our things about me. Then I met Craigie. He took me home one night when I got drunk, and stuck with me, a dour homesick Scot, mournful enough even for me."

"Weren't your parents worried?"

"They worked like beavers, not very successfully, until they hit upon the plan of sending me abroad. It didn't seem a bad idea. Father had vast mining interests and produced a lot of fieldwork. It was only a matter of time before they'd sack me from my academic job in a laboratory, so I departed, accompanied by Craigie, to take up Herculean labours in portions of the earth not usually inhabited by man."

"That was a wise move."

"Psychologically, yes. I did good work and fulfilled their wildest hopes commercially, but when I had finished the preliminary job I went down sick, miles from anywhere. Craigie, who'd had a spell as medical orderly, nursed me devotedly and pulled me through; but when they brought me home, it was found I had some wretched

tropical disease, with no known cure. I did respond to the
treatment which they gave me. I was pretty tough in
those days. Then I was told it might recur, and if it did,
the outlook wasn't bright. I was recommended to stay
near my doctors, give up all work, and play the invalid.
But as I had no interest in prolonging life on such terms,
I preferred to complete my task and damn the rest. In
any case, at that age, you can't envisage pain and decay.
Imagination doesn't stretch so far. You're either dead or
well."

"You went back to the tropics?"

"Immediately, and poor Craigie too. I was interested,
you see, and challenged. I knew that I was near to
something big, and so I was. And I had even written it up
before I had my next attack. This time I was flown home
*in extremis*. I survived, but that's about all. Life soon
became a sort of horror comic; an endless stretch of pain
and uselessness. But I had made my discovery—and the
firm a mint of money—and I had to be content with that.
I little thought I would gain new distinction as a human
Rhesus monkey, but by the time they stumbled on this
drug, I hadn't much to lose. Nor was there any chance of
lasting out till the cure was properly screened. The rest
you know. I surprised even the optimists; I'm the hope of
undeveloped countries. I can easily find excuse for self-
importance, but delight and gratitude are rather more
clusive."

"You could be grateful that the worst is over. After
hell, even limbo has its points."

"A negative consolation," said Alastair, "and one I like
less now than I did once."

There was very little sense in saying formal things,

repeating them in rather different terms. For the past becomes ingrown, as I well knew, and Alastair's spirit company seemed worse than mine. I felt a new affection for my crew. They had voices, faces, anyway. They weren't perfect angels like the lost wife. They had no greedy grip on Alastair.

Yet she had called them here and they were watching. I pushed the thought aside and looked up at the clock. Time always drags when you would have it hurry. I couldn't stay now till the bus. I could sit by the seashore and work this out. I daren't stay here with Alastair. Lucky, I'd been discreet—thank God for this disguise— no one need ever know how near I'd been to foolishness.

# 10

## The Shepherd's Crook

"AFTER THAT MASSIVE dose of life history, a drink seems to be indicated." Alastair had retrieved his smile, though his manner was still brusque. He poured out two whiskies, his own nearly neat. I noticed that he drank it in one gulp.

"I was thinking that I really ought to go. You've had enough of me."

"Nonsense. It's early yet. The trouble is I've bored you stiff. I won't offend again. But we're due for something just a bit more cheerful. Shall we discuss your ill-assorted lovers?"

The biter bit. My favourite counter-topic turned against me. I was off Deborahs for the moment, even my own shorn lamb. Had I known her millions and her virtue were in dire peril, I doubt if I'd have moved a foot to save her. I haven't an exemplary character.

"You're right," said Alastair. "Of course you are. One forgets that youth is quite so vulnerable, and girls are far more innocent at that age than most people pretend. It's asking too much of a child like that to make a judgment between sheep and goats. I could find out who her trustees are, I suppose. It might be as well to know."

He sounded vastly sympathetic; you could have said nostalgic. It crossed my mind a man of habit could find here a repeat of the same pattern. A nice pretty child whose name was Deborah. A final irony if Alastair should be the means of ousting cousin Peter.

I wouldn't stoop to playing dog in the manger like the first Mrs. Forres. And if a rebound could be engineered, the orphan child might possibly veer towards a father figure. They had the same background, and money ceased to matter. Her name would echo slightly just at first, but soon he'd hardly know the difference.

This was the sort of discipline I understood and about the first thing that made sense this evening. Let him talk on. I didn't care. He sounded most paternal.

Paternal! Yes, the word stuck in my daft wandering mind. Like a father. That was it. The way he knocked his pipe against the fireplace or changed mood from tenderness to anger. That consciousness of latent passion and despair, masked by a careless manner. A Gael, of course; we're all a bit like that, but I had seen a likeness and must face it.

As well that frost had come early. An Oedipus complex would have been just too much. That's why I liked his black hair and his eyebrows and obeyed him in command and caress. If there was any resemblance at all, I'd better get him right out my system. And there was. Hadn't

Father always said that Mother was a sort of saint, a view not shared by Nurse and Miss Lamont?

The same story really, but the baby girl lived on and bore the brunt of it.

Till in her turn it was she who failed him.

I was using Alastair to keep him off—to make him flesh and blood.

I was a coward and deserved my fate.

"You're very pensive. Have you heard a word I've said?"

"You were talking about Deborah Mansfield."

"Some time ago. You look strange again. Don't stare like that. The light's gone out of your eyes. Is this the way to put it back again?"

It was queer. This time he had only to touch me and I struggled like a wild beast. Maybe I clawed or something, like I used to, against what seemed abomination. The result was that he lost his new-found temper and set out to master me, which of course was the worst thing he could have done. His eyes blazed and his whole body matched their mood. The daemon chained inside him now escaped, and we two met head-on.

"I hate you!" I gasped. "Hate you! How dare you touch me—you! Let me go, damn you—let me go! Who the hell do you think you are? Who do you think I am? A bawd to smuggle in through the back door? The best of a bloody awful bunch? With your fine new health and vigour, do your weeks seem overlong without a woman? But you've made the wrong choice. You need a tramp, not me."

"I know exactly what I need."

"I'm not an opiate either—a cure to satisfy male vanity or dull the jagged edges. I have some pride left, God knows why, and I'll keep it for myself. I may have been an actress and sex symbol, but myself I don't go cheap and never will."

"Darling, you're crying!"

"I am not!" Despite the fact my tears poured down. "You keep your hands off me. I can't stand it."

"Oh, my poor, idiotic love. Come here, for goodness' sake, and tell me what's the matter. Your virtue isn't hanging by a thread surely? You won't go cheap with me. This time you'd better have my handkerchief, and I think my shoulder too."

"You'd no right to make love to me like that."

"Perhaps not, till you've told me what is wrong."

"Nothing and everything. I think I'm going mad. You stopped me yesterday. Please stop me now."

He opened his jacket merely and laid my head against a soft, smooth shirt. He held me very close and stroked my hair.

"This isn't yesterday," he said.

It was true. It didn't matter any more that I should cry in front of him. In any case I couldn't stop. I was too tired to try. It was the reckoning. I couldn't hold *them* off any longer. There had been one shocking moment when they tore me apart, so that now I was not whole any longer.

"I had no idea that it would hurt like this. I can't stand it. I ought to have cried long ago, when it was natural. I can't catch up now ever—ever."

"You get it out of your system. You'll feel better."

"I don't suppose I will. I'll feel shamed. To talk to you in such a way, and now this."

"But you're funny in a rage, and I like you in my arms, so you needn't apologize, wee hedgehog."

I soaked his shirt, I sobbed and gulped. The whole thing was absurd. From time to time I would burst out with a statement just as incomprehensible as Mandarin Chinese. Alastair mostly did not attempt an answer but went on soothing me. And slowly there was a lightening which led to more articulate speech. Nonsense, perhaps, but easing, so I didn't care.

"I despise puppets. But you have to start again where you leave off. Then you can't find the right place. It's gone and you're nowhere. No one. I haven't even got a name any more."

"You'll find one. Meanwhile you're my nut-brown maiden. I expect you're in the wood-of-no-names, like the other Alice."

"I'm like her, yes. Even time goes backwards and jumps about."

"It'll settle. Leave it alone. I think you're fighting it."

"I have to. To keep *them* away, you know. They won't leave me alone. I think I have a persecution complex. When I had real work to do, they kept away."

"Who are *they?*"

That pulled me up enough to find some cunning.

"At any rate, I talk like a lunatic," I said.

"Better than bottling up and pushing down the cork. You need a psychoanalyst, my love."

"I do not. I don't girn and gabble out my bothers. I'd rather have a breakdown!"

I think he was relieved at my tone, and so, to tell the truth, was I. I began to mop my eyes ferociously and swallow hard, and he gave me a drink which knocked me straight.

It was like coming into a well-lit room after long labyrinths of dark. How strange that he should give me peace, when he had none. There were no words to thank him for standing by me when I was afraid, for offering me his plaid in the storm.

The rest was just a blur—that drink perhaps. I remember growing emptier and emptier and not minding. I could see myself a shape of atoms, hovering together. It seemed a proper thing to be. My head dropped, my eyes closed, and I went to sleep against him. Indeed, the next thing I recall was his gentle shaking.

"I'd far rather keep you here," he said, "but your bus is nearly due, so we'd better observe the proprieties."

I was still rather vague. It seemed odd to go down to Holly Bank at this time of night. I wondered what Miss Lamont would have thought of Alastair. Not that she knew a great deal about men.

As long as he was near me, I was calm, but the parting left me dazed and incredulous. James, luckily, had gone to bed, and I went straight upstairs. It was then the long day was photographed across my mind, a sequence of total unreality. I couldn't have behaved like that. I couldn't. A snivelling thing; an object of compassion . . .

I couldn't even do the simplest thing. I lay down like a child with all my clothes on and fell into a sleep like a coma. It washed over me like flood water, drowning guilt and care. And I dreamed a dream which used to be a nightmare—but this time nothing happened. I've never known such wonderful relief.

The next morning I woke with heavy eyes and a queer nervous flutter in my solar plexus. Apart from that, nothing was patently amiss. I was still very tired and thoroughly lackluster. I seemed to have a combined hangover from drink and emotion. I also felt a strong disinclination ever to see Alastair or Castle Rannoch as long as I lived. To find James munching toast and marmalade was reassuring.

"Good film? Which category?"

"Tear-jerker," I replied, approaching truth.

"How tedious. Is that why you look so tired?"

"Do I? I'm getting rustic. Not used to long days and late nights."

"And how do you intend to pass the Sabbath? Are you a pillar of the Christian faith?"

"It's time I did some work."

"I also, but experience, often bitter, has proved the sound of busy typing is ungrateful to the highland ear on Sundays. Our neighbours are Wee Frees, Auld Lichts, or some such brotherhood."

I had no mind to attend the kirk and expose my familiar profile through a long sermon. Yet mooning round the house without occupation was unwise and might well prove depressing.

But soon after breakfast, fate stepped in, in the shape of Catherine Macdonald. She telephoned, and I welcomed such a symbol of neutrality.

"How lovely to hear from you," I said.

"You remember those people we discussed?"

"I saw them yesterday."

"So did I. If you are Sherlock, I'm your Watson, the tortoise of the partnership."

I'd forgotten one talked riddles on an open line to quell the keepers of the grapevine.

"You know my methods, Watson," I supplied to gain time and expertise.

"Well, mine are plodding. No brilliant deductions but slow and sure results. Would it interest you to compare notes? Turn Ilsafeccan into Baker Street?"

"But yes."

"Good! Are you free today, by any chance?"

I said, with sudden hope, that I was.

"Because I think we ought to talk things over soon. The amatory chart is rising. Anyhow, Sundays can be boring."

"I'm bored," I admitted candidly.

"Then you must come to lunch and tea and have a real outing."

"Theoretically there's nothing I'd like better, but though I may yet catch the Sunday bus—what can I do at Stranach?"

"You mean transport? Didn't I say? That's fixed from door to door. Would half-past ten be too early? Your chauffeur has to make another call."

I promised to be ready and rang off feeling more cheerful. I'd fooled Robin once; I'd fool him twice. Besides, Miss Rayner's Sunday best had a matching hat, enough to put off any man's inspection.

James was surprised to learn about my programme. I explained the Macdonalds, but he was still amazed our chance acquaintance should lead to hospitality. However, he was meditating madly, so he only raised his stubbly eyebrows.

"My dear Alice, you are a most successful social climber. One can only trust you don't fall down and bark your shins. Give the McD of A my kind regards, though perhaps he will not deign to accept them."

"I thought him harmless and she charming."

"I expect you have a predilection for the landed gentry."

"Or don't suffer from inferiority a lot," I countered drily. He had a nice grin, James.

I waited, rather keyed up, expecting Robin, but the car which arrived on the minute proved to be a Jag. So what was I to do? I peered through the curtains at Alastair, superbly tailored in Glen Urquhart, and my heart sank to my half-brogued shoes.

"Are you Miss Rayner?" As I opened the door, the voice was loud enough to drift through all the neighbours' windows.

"Yes," I said meekly, feeling like a fool. Oh, Lord! What a miscalculation!

"I understand you want a lift to Ilsafeccan. I'm lunching there as well."

I could only agree. The Walter Gairs were on their way to kirk and took great interest in the conversation.

So I said goodbye to James and bundled in.

We drove away. I scarcely breathed until we'd left the village safely behind; and I must have glared at Alastair, for he crinkled those wretched eyes at me.

"It will enhance your position in Glenshael," he said. "To lunch with the MacDonalds of Anacher gives a seal of respectability. You're made, my dear. You're Caesar's wife at last."

"I didn't expect you," I said sullenly.

"I didn't think you would."

"I suppose that you arranged all this."

"Well, you're wrong. I merely took advantage of circumstances. When Catherine Macdonald rang me up, I did try to refuse, until I heard that you were asked too, and then I gave in gracefully."

"I should have thought you needed a rest from my company."

"Ach, what a face! Relax, Miss Rayner. It's a fine morning, love. The snail's on the thorn and God knows what larks are doing. Winds blow south, winds blow north—while we two keep together. I feel poetic."

"So it appears," I said.

"Never mind, love, you'll have an excellent luncheon to improve your temper, and I know fine what that means to you."

"You're incorrigible, Alastair." I smiled at last. "I suppose that I must grin and bear it. Incidentally, do the Macdonalds know we've met each other?"

"I didn't tell them. I find I become clandestine with you. You're not a good influence. Not that it matters. We can introduce ourselves on the journey. *Alice, the pudding: the pudding, Alice!* Ought we to seal it with a kiss?"

"You dare! Keep your eyes on the road."

"How does it happen you know them?"

I explained the Rannoch-Mansfield connection, which made Alastair laugh.

"Your whole social life revolves round those two."

"I know it does. It's funny. Even you."

"But we ourselves will leave them till we reach Ilsafeccan. Darling, where did you get that awful hat? Do take
it off. With your organizing tendencies, you'll end up with
a Girl Guide troop if you wear atrocities like that."

He whistled as we drove through Stranach. We went
less cautiously today. The hood was down and his hair
was tumbled. In view of the appalling draught, I removed
both hat and wig.

"Hello, nut-brown maid." He smiled. "I've never
known a girl with false hair."

"Well, I've often worn it. It saves a lot of trouble.
When I was on the stage, I had a pile of fancy styles and
colours. I collected them."

"You'll go bald," he said lazily.

"Alastair, I will not! How dare you say so?"

"And serve you right," he added.

It was strange to approach Anacher again.

"What a huge dam!" I said.

"Our host's handiwork. Anacher was the engineer in
charge."

"Really? How ironic. And how progressive! I wonder if
James knows. He thinks that highland gentlemen are
parasites."

"Often they are. The Rannochs are a good example.
Perhaps young Deborah's friend is one after all. They
batten on rich wives."

He had pulled up above the valley, presumably so we
could study civil engineering. I had one of my swift
dislikes for him.

"I thought you had an errand somewhere. Here?"

"You could say so, love. I wanted a long time with you, and if we go on at this rate we'll get there far too early."

"You're full of tricks," I snapped at him. "I suppose you think you're clever."

"Not really. Though it is a relief to find you back on form. I worried half the night about you."

"I don't see why you should."

"It felt all wrong to take you back to Bywater in such a state. The man's a clot anyway. I kept waking up imagining the worst. An overdose of sleeping tablets was one nightmare, deliberately or accidentally, because I'd laced your drink. You looked appalling—almost fey. And I seemed to be responsible."

"You weren't, Alastair. It was just accumulation of some sort. And as for your horrors, they were quite unnecessary. I flaked out at once."

"I hoped you would, but then I told myself you'd never wish to set eyes on me again."

"I did feel that."

"So the sooner that we met again, the better—and here we are."

And round went his arm once again.

"What were you saying about Rannochs and rich wives?" I forced myself to say to starch my resolution.

"I did a survey once," he replied contentedly. "When I took down the library shelves, I found a lot of old papers and, having nothing else to do, studied the Rannochs sociologically What a weird bunch! Completely irresponsible, extravagant, and obviously unbalanced."

"Ought you to look at other people's papers?" I asked coldly.

"I don't see why not. Besides, I'd promised when I

bought the place to look out for information everywhere. It was when Lady Menzies was alive and they still hoped to find the girl. I turned up nothing new on her, but as there was a lot of clan history there I duly sent them off to the old man in Lombard Street."

"Lombard Street?" It reminded me of Peter.

"Off it, I should say. Office of the Rannochs' English agent, an exiled Scot with highland mania who keeps in touch for love."

"Alastair." My resentment had dispersed with this unexpected information. "Peter told Deborah he worked in Lombard Street. Do you think that's the connection? He could have been a clerk to this agent man and armed himself with heaps of information."

"Something like that must have happened, for I doubt if he picked it up round here. The local people close up like clams when you mention Aillie Rannoch. I shouldn't do so in front of Anacher, for instance. It is a social *gaffe*. The wife doesn't matter. She's a foreigner."

"Do you know them well?"

"As well as I know anyone round here, which isn't intimately. It's only recently I've come back into circulation. I don't mind Macdonald. We speak the same language approximately, and she is rather kind. But I don't like folk, as well you know, and they're too hospitable for my taste. When they ask me over, then I have to ask them back."

"It'll do you good to go out."

"I'd far rather play truant. Just the two of us instead of troops of people. And a whole long day ahead. Wouldn't you like that too?"

"And miss my lunch?"

"Ach, I'd forgotten. Our appetites are different. But you have to wait an hour. I haven't."

"Alastair, this is a public highway, not private grounds!"

"And you have to contribute towards my rehabilitation."

A grand way for saying a simple thing.

It was a golden morning on the hill, and we above the whole world, and ourselves. Up till then, and afterwards, a host of problems dogged me, so it was good to be a bit weary and my mind rather blank. I could smell the wild thyme in the hot sun, for it was like high summer. We both nearly fell asleep.

Even Alastair kept yawning.

"A rationing system, love, might suit us better. We do go headlong. You know I have grown so self-centered, it's exhausting to consider other people."

"You don't have to consider me."

"But I enjoy it, in small doses. It's like playing mental squash—very limbering but you are stiff next day."

"Ach, what a pretty compliment!" I said, obeying an overpowering impulse to trace the contour of his nose.

It was the first time I allowed myself to pretend, just for a little while, that I belonged to Alastair—and he to me. The fact that I knew it must be make-believe added a poignant pleasure to the game.

# 11

## The
## Highland Reel

A HIGHLY POLISHED table was laid with heavy silver. Catherine had eased up the room with glazed chintz, but tradition still predominated and change merged into the unchanging. As a hostess, Catherine was preferable. Elizabeth Macdonald had always disapproved of me.

"You'll eat the fat I've given you, Ilsafeccan," said Robin, sounding just like his father, "or take a skelping. Understand?"

The small boy glowered and made no answer. I smiled to myself. He could not know that he was continuity. He even had his father's mute rebellion.

"You haven't given him too much, Robin?" Catherine was loving and weak-minded over children.

"No, I have not," replied her husband; and that, it seemed, was that.

I had almost forgotten Sunday lunch, that punctuating feature of a highland childhood. The massive sirloin, the bouffant batter, the enormous piles of vegetables. The half-trained table maid had gone for good, but the ceremony, it seemed, remained. I was back in rural Scotland, where a chicken or a curry would have broken the Sabbath, and where carving was a science and an art.

"Let me give you some more undercut, Miss Rayner." I was glad he didn't press *me* to eat fat. But my plate was so high-piled by now, it daunted even me, though I assured the world in general all was delicious.

Catherine was spooning mash and gravy down a pretty little minx in a highchair. A dog's head lay upon my foot beneath the table. The few domesticated friends I had in London had often invited me to cold meat at the weekend, but they'd drink till three and then forget to eat at all. No wonder they divorced or reared delinquents. Such gatherings as these were anchors. These children were luckier than they knew.

"I suppose I could afford to plant ten acres," Robin was saying rather doubtfully.

"Not worth it," answered Alastair. "The subsoil here's too poor."

"Still, one likes to plow back a little. Kinlochanacher could stand some trees."

The Master of Ilsafeccan, having cleaned his plate and hit his sister with a bread pellet, stared hard at the men talking but kept his mouth shut. He would recall them in the years to come when he was thinking about planting too.

"He's the image of his father," I observed to my hostess. It was like giving her a medal on a gold plate, but

I wondered how she'd fare with two of them, or perhaps even more.

After lunch the menfolk disappeared and the children were disposed of for their good. Catherine and I were left alone with deck chairs by the lochside.

"Heavenly place!" I remarked in my best English, my eyes lifted to the hills of Anacher in proper tourist fashion.

"Yes, it is, rather." She dismissed the subject impatiently. It was old stuff. "I hope it was all right, by the way, about Alastair. I should perhaps have warned you. People are sometimes scared of him. He can be very saturnine."

"It was most kind of him to bring me over."

"He's not bad really. We rather like him. Mind you, he's different today. He was quite unusually forthcoming, and I heard him laugh—*twice*."

"Is that so extraordinary?"

"Good gracious, yes. I've never known him laugh before, and he smiles as if it hurt him. But again, not today. Did you notice how his eyes crinkled? He's not unattractive."

To me it seemed a lukewarm comment, but I could not see straight with Alastair. Catherine chattered on. Her lot, I thought, had fallen in fair places. She had everything girls dream about: a handsome husband, an enchanting house, and two fine healthy bairns for good measure. It ought to be enough for anyone, but I saw the limitations. In a place like Anacher, a lust grows on you for a cosy gossip. The men are always busy and can't work up much interest in shredding personalities, which is a very female ploy besides. Poor Catherine was hungry for the teacup world, and I was only sorry she should focus upon Alastair.

"We got on very well," I replied to her renewed enquiries, determined soon to head her off. "You see, we found a subject of conversation. Mr. Forres travelled up with me on the same train, and he recognized my protégée. He says she's Deborah Mansfield, the millionairess."

"Deborah Mansfield? How exciting!" The diversion was successful indeed. "But Lord! It makes it more complicated. I wish I'd known this yesterday. I've spoken to her. I'd lost Steenie and gone in search of him, when I met the two of them, amorous on the hill. Love, sandwiches, the lot. I decided it was too good an opportunity to miss, so I hove up and asked them if they'd seen a small boy around. I told them who I was, and Peter came over very civil. A crashing snob—it's nearly pathological."

"I have that impression too."

"He cadged an invitation to tea, so I played. She wasn't at all keen, but she's a good-natured child and she could see we pleased him. When Robin turned up, it was even worse. He froze on like a limpet and talked far too much about highland traditions, though no word of the Rannochs."

"How did your husband respond?"

"Like an angel—or do I mean devil? A sort of glint came in his eye which I knew boded trouble for the Monarch. By tea time the poor chap was literally on his knees. You felt if Robin slapped him on the back once more, he'd fall forwards, and his head was so full of rubbish he was drunk with it. I'm afraid my husband has a sadist streak and a most odd sense of humour."

"What is she like?"

"A sweetie really. I liked her very much. She's nice, though she is rather mannered. I mean we discussed Schönberg and the twelve-tone scale, just like a Sunday paper. I see now that it could be a defense mechanism. She doesn't want to be an empty-headed heiress, all frivolity. I don't go much beyond Beethoven, and like a dominant in both males and scales. But that's all very superficial. At her first glimpse of my Catriona I saw the real person. She adores babies, really and truly. Good with them too. If she had to earn her living the hard way, she'd make an excellent nanny."

"Your Catriona is a very pretty child," I pointed out.

"How nice of you to say so, but you don't yearn to hug her, do you? Deborah did. A mum can always differentiate between the bored and the enraptured. I gave full marks to Deborah; you are a poor halfway; then there are folk like Alastair who shudder when they see a toddler."

"Men tend to be awkward with the very young," I said uneasily.

"With Catriona? She ought to have been called Lolita. And anyhow he's just as bad with Steenie. He used to look abominably ill and wince at every noise. I think, if he's taken to laughing, I must reform him. He must appreciate my young a little more."

"No!" I said sharply, horrified at this development.

"Why not? I love annoying bachelors and teasing them."

"Mr. Forres lost his wife and baby daughter. Rather more complex." I felt I was betraying a confidence, but I wasn't going to have Alastair hurt by a stupid girl.

"I didn't know that." Catherine stared at me, certainly shocked, but even more curious than before. "Thanks for telling me. I might have put my foot in it. How do you know?"

I wished I hadn't spoken.

"His wife died years ago," I added. "Most people have forgotten."

"Did he tell you himself? How odd. And yet, you're that kind of a person. I don't know why. Except perhaps that you're neither old nor young, yet somehow both. I'm talking nonsense, but it's somehow truth. You're an enigma, that's what you are."

"To get back to Deborah," I said hastily, "I've decided that we need a rival."

"Where to find one? Your boss and Alastair are the only eligible males for miles around, and they won't do. A rival must outclass Peter at his own game."

"Not necessarily. The time might come when she's had a surfeit of tartan and longs for the ordinary and calculable. What we need for this plot is a boy-next-door."

"How funny you should say that. I have the impression, very vague, she's run away from someone. Perhaps a suitor in the south. It's far more common to escape people than mere environment, and she doesn't seem to have any family. She thinks Peter exciting and original, which suggests the other, if he does exist, is deadly dull. I am deducing too!"

"If we assumed the suitor was not imagination," I said thoughtfully, "what next?"

"We must extricate her from Peter's spell."

"God knows how. It would be difficult enough if we really knew the girl. As it is, she's a sort of plaything for us all."

"Not for me," said Catherine with quiet dignity. "I happen to be really concerned. You see, I married the wrong man when I was her age, and believe me, I'd go to any lengths to stop a young girl making the same mistake. It's hell, Miss Rayner. It's difficult to get over. But I was lucky, and because of that I owe life a vast debt. I want to do for others what was done for me, or I don't deserve my happiness should last. Also, I was spared a Rannoch. Odd how that name couples in my mind with insecurity."

"Why on earth?"

"Childish jealousy. I say it with shame. Robin always swears he never looked at anyone but me. A likely story! Not that I mind. Except for Aillie Rannoch, the girl who haunts Glenshael. Everyone mourns her so laboriously but she sounds a prize bitch to me."

"I agree. A ghastly child," I said demurely.

"Well, I think so. But Robin doesn't. His eyes light up when we discuss her, which is not very often fortunately. He pretends that he was sorry for her—poor wee Aillie! He was half in love with her—a woman knows."

"Good thing she's dead," I put in cheerfully.

"Is she? Not that I hope so, but I'd prefer her to keep away from here. It's not that I don't trust Robin, but she sounds exactly the sort of person to set a peaceful society by the ears, and there aren't so many feuds and furors these days."

The proverbial reservations about the absent and dead did not, I thought wryly, apply to me. The things that people said about Aillie Rannoch! I seldom heard much good of myself.

Mind you, I sympathized with Catherine. I noticed over tea, when we touched upon the Rannochs, that

Robin never mentioned me. Nothing is more irritating than deliberate silence on one subject, especially a member of the opposite sex. Catherine was far too generous to be jealous, but she was also human.

I enjoyed my day, but strain was inevitable. It was a relief to be alone with Alastair. In his car I relaxed and was myself.

"Nice people," I said lazily.

"Improving. When I first used to visit them, it was an ordeal. Catherine would gaze at her lord as though he'd just stepped off a cloud, while he resented even a warm handshake. Such surfeits of interworship are tedious to an outsider."

"Poor misanthropic Alastair! Personally I like to see folk in that plight. People are less and less demonstrative. Why shouldn't married pairs behave like lovers? It's hard on children too, who understand the cuff and the caress but dread detached, intelligent handling. I can still remember the horrors of being lectured with sublimated affection."

"Did anyone really waste time lecturing you?"

"Yes, but I didn't listen."

"And I suppose you approve of Anacher child welfare? Calling a small boy by his title and brandishing the rod?"

"The proof of the pudding—he had charming manners, which properly brought-up children seem to lack. I'll tell you this, Alastair, if my London friends ever entrusted their dear offspring to me, I'd skelp them to a standstill."

"And break their spirits?"

"Ach, it takes more than that. When I was wee I seldom sat down comfortably, but no one broke my spirit, I am thinking."

We drove on in pleasant silence. I was no longer tired, though a thought listless. If I often spent days with Alastair, life, I knew, would be hell without him. His companionship was more demoralizing than his grander flights.

I looked sideways at him. The evening light played on his face to wipe out years and cares. "Not unattractive," I remembered. What a thing to say to me!

"A penny for them, love."

"I was still thinking about the Macdonalds," I lied promptly. "It's mean to laugh at them. She's wonderfully content, I think, and he patently adores her and always will."

"Of course. He chose her, didn't he? Not a man who would admit himself mistaken. Are you envious? You needn't be. If you were in her shoes, there'd soon be murder. He'd try and keep you in your proper place, and you'd never understand where that was. You need someone to henpeck. You'll never make a docile wife."

"I should say Catherine maneuvers him just as she pleases."

"But you couldn't. You're too stiff-necked."

"Does that mean I'm unfeminine?"

"It means that you're *you*."

He was right. All very sad, but common sense, and no great loss to Alastair. I was no ideal helpmate. Imagine saying "yes" and "no," all meek and mild, and always being what some man expected. Some man? One man. I looked at him again. Poor stuff for henpecking, I thought. That jaw line knew its business; that mouth could harden to immense decision. Made long ago; the right girl at the right time. He'd lost her, true, but only superficially, so it no longer mattered if the choice were random. Otherwise I might have settled for maneuvering too, had the gains been worth the strategy.

I was myself, for better or for worse, conscious of basic elements which could not be reshaped. I'd never been an understudy or compromised with two-bit parts. I'd star or nothing, and I'd pick my roles. A docile wife was right out of my range, though more interesting than the second string. Mistress might be more suitable; not a long run but honest while it lasted. What a daft thought! Could this be Miss Lamont's sin of self-indulgence? Deadly for sure, probably deadening too, but at the reckoning better than stupidity.

"Today," said Alastair, "we've missed the sunset. But the moon is rising. I like nocturnes. Time to stop."

"I notice that you don't consult me."

"Have I put notions in your head? Could it be you feel downtrodden?"

"You yourself complain of Anacher's high hand, but you're the same exactly."

"I'm not, you know. I prefer balance; and the harder to achieve, the more interesting I find it. The Anachers of life are easily suited. They demand adoration, and they mostly get it."

"And what do you demand?"

"Challenge, I think. Though that's simplification."

He scooped me up, this time in a bear-hug.

"You look pensive. Would you prefer it if I treated you like Dresden china?"

"I see no reason why you should."

"Perhaps because you have a Dresden nose. It's pretty.

How do you contrive, love, to look so dreich with all your assets?"

"You don't behave as if I did."

"But you change alone with me. I find it very gratifying when you drop your spidery lashes over your green eyes. . . ."

"They are not green."

"But they are. A sort of muddy green."

"Like your wretched pond, I'm thinking."

"A little, and now I come to think of it, you are like a water lily."

"*Nymphaea alba* or *Nuphar lutea?*" I asked politely.

And the conversation ended most abruptly.

Long after midnight I lay wide awake, remembering the evening behind.

The moon was near the full, let any moon be my reminder. But this one, he said, belonged to me.

Later, we wandered down Glen Anacher. He took my hand; that's all. A rowan tree was etched against the silvered sky; a dog-fox ran across the turf, not knowing we were there. He said we mustn't speak—that silence had more value. And words did seem inadequate for sure. A curious shyness came on both of us. It was a night of no demands, no offers—a strange vignette of peace.

A sort of glimpse of truth came in the quiet. He wasn't fooling, which made matters worse. He'd said I challenged him. To what? To real unhappiness and loss of all we'd found? I wouldn't henpeck, I'd claw and rip at my poor predecessor. Strangle out lies to feed my ego, and slowly kill the thing I loved and needed. Poor Alastair, whose integrity and twisted kindness sat on him so well.

He was a lonely man, who needed true affection more than most and wouldn't put up with a prize bitch very long. For I knew that I was jealous, exacting, probably malicious. I was proud, in the Bible sense—a haughty spirit bent upon destruction.

But I would not destroy Alastair. Only the best was good enough for him.

# 12

## The Yellow-Haired Laddie

JAMES'S MEDITATIONS BORE a crop of chapters, which kept me busy all next day. It was a chance to moor my mind. I don't mull over things already settled.

It was time I left Glenshael. I only had to work out when and how. It was absurd; it was a pity. I belonged here; the best of the highland year lay ahead. Damn Alastair! Everything else went well.

No real depression. I had solved my true dilemma. It was good to be emancipated from the past. The present might be awkward and the future drab, but all seemed quite negotiable and near the surface. Then too, it was gratifying that Alastair should be a problem. He might have thought me awful, which I was. A shame he couldn't know about my noble nature. It impressed me very much myself.

When the day's stint was done and dinner over, I curled up by the fire, happy in James's company. His fisher jersey needed washing, his teenage jeans were not flattering, but what a change from handsome woman plaguers!

I was knitting. I'd never finished anything, even under Nurse's eye in the old days. My present progress showed how much I had improved in steadiness of character, or was it merely that a foot or two of ribbing was necessary to the part of Alice Rayner?

James switched on the Third Programme and adjusted his concert pose, head bowed in hand, all beatific concentration. Myself, I winced. Hindemith rampant, double-canned! He has his own cacophonies without the atmospherics of Glenshael. *Mathis der Mahler* was about quarter through when Donaldina, in her coat, pushed in a strange man before departing. He stood there lost and overpowered.

I put him in the early twenties and his butter-coloured hair was strong and thick, matching his sturdy shoulders and pugnacious face. His clothes were old and ready-made, but he had a very scrubbed look. Shoes, highly polished and square-toed; collar and tie, and even waistcoat. He shrieked convention to Bohemian Holly Bank and brought commuters' London to Glenshael.

James at last switched off Hindemith unwillingly.

"I do not think I have the pleasure of your name, sir," he remarked with a ponderous, Johnsonian air.

"I'm David Gregory," the boy answered. "Not that it will convey a thing to you."

"No," replied James unhelpfully. Like Alastair, he hated evening visitors.

"I'm related to Lord Mantum," David Gregory continued firmly. "My mother, actually, is Lady Mantum's cousin. So I'm staying at Anacher House, and Lady Mantum suggested to my mother that I should look you up."

"I can't imagine why, though I am honoured that the Mantums should remember the existence of a poor benighted scribbler."

"But I'm most interested to find that you live here. I do write myself, actually."

"A little often goes a long way," said James, unimpressed. He really was a bit hard on the poor lad.

"Do sit down, Mr. Gregory," I intercepted. "I'm Alice Rayner, Mr. Bywater's secretary. I didn't realize that Lord Mantum had opened up Anacher House so early in the year."

"It's not exactly open. I had an appendix—I'm on sick leave, and I needed somewhere to convalesce."

"When you say you write," James interrupted, "I conclude you scrape the gutters for your illustrious relative by marriage. Are you here to look for copy?"

"No, sir, I'm not a journalist. Actually I'm in the Foreign Office. Only I've always felt I could write a novel, so it's tremendously interesting to meet you."

"A diplomat and C. P. Snow manqué. If you've come to me for literary advice, Mr. Gregory, I'll not detain you. Stick to the Foreign Office, and stick hard. You may not make ambassador, but the income's regular."

"James, don't be so discouraging! Mr. Gregory's only trying to be polite. He's on his own in Anacher House, which is enough to drive him out even to visit you. It's a lonely, dismal sort of place."

"Certainly is," agreed the boy. "The evenings in particular are very boring, so I take out the car and drive
around."

"But we are boring too, my dear boy."

"Not to me, sir. You've no idea how I enjoyed reading
*Naked on My Pavement*."

James, I suspected, chose his titles tongue in cheek to
suit this sort of situation and trap too glib admirers into
schoolboy humour. Poor David blushed belatedly, and
being so fair, he did it thoroughly. Again I rushed in to
help.

"Are you a highland addict, Mr. Gregory?"

"Not particularly. I like Devon and Cornwall, though
up here is very fascinating, of course, when you get to
know the ropes. I've heard a lot about this part of the
world from a friend of mine, who's absolutely crazy on
it."

"Some people are."

"She's always planning holidays in Scotland, saying
how marvellous it is. As a matter of fact, I wondered
whether she was up here at present."

At last I felt I had some clue to him. I'd been conscious
all along he was leading in some specific direction.

"Nice if she were," I murmured. "It would be more fun
if you had a friend near by."

He looked relieved. "Yes, it would. Of course I'm only
guessing. When I came out of hospital, you see, she'd
gone away. It would be a piece of luck if she were here."

"But surely you could find out? Couldn't anybody tell
you where she'd gone?"

"It does sound a bit odd, but no! The housekeeper
thought she was with a school friend, whom I happened

to know too, but when I telephoned they'd had no word from her. And the cousin she lives with had gone abroad. It's frightfully complicated."

It was all too easy to think of Deborah; enough, at least, to make me curious and guarded.

"There aren't so many places open," I said. "Quite simple to check surely? Ring them all up in turn."

"I have, more or less, but they've no Miss Mansfield. The Stranach Hotel, for instance. She's often talked about it, which is rather why I chose Anacher as my headquarters."

"You came to look for her—specifically?"

"In a manner of speaking, yes."

"Would she have any reason to have changed her name? Sounds odd, but people sometimes do on holiday. If by any chance she were the famous Deborah Mansfield, for instance, she'd be wise to go incognito. The reporters are always at her heels, particularly Lord Mantum's."

"Good grief! I never thought of that. But I don't expect Mother said anything. Actually she is Deborah Mansfield. I've known her all my life."

A boy-next-door, and what on earth to do about him? He was obviously a suitor of some sort and with enough intuition to trace her to the highlands. Yet at the same time, it had not occurred to the simple soul she'd cover up her tracks. This was no match for the more devious mind of Mr. Peter Rannoch. He seemed so little suited to the situation, I continued to move with caution.

"Poor child, I often read about her in the papers. She must be harried, a natural prey to fortune hunters."

"That's a polite word for the sort of riffraff who hang

round her nowadays," snorted David. "The dregs of café society, arty-crafty parasites, and every titled drip with a weak chin and an unpaid tailor's bill. And that cousin of hers encourages them. Partly through vanity to make a good match for her on paper, partly to shrug off the responsibility as soon as possible. And she has the audacity to tell Deb that I'm on the make."

I looked him up and down again; correct, genteel, and shabby. You could see the cousin's point.

"It's understandable, I suppose," I said aloud, though quite sympathetically. "For in your line of work, money is always very useful, I've been told."

"And so has Deb!" The fact that he took my intrusion in his stride argued advanced worry of some sort. "But she ought to have the sense to see I would still want her if she hadn't got a penny. She's known me long enough to trust me, after all."

"Sorry to harp—but have you any money of your own?"

"A little, but since my father died we're not well off. We never were in the Mansfield bracket anyhow. But as I told her, I at least have a career. It won't always be so ill-balanced."

"By which I gather you've already offered."

"I have and been refused. I don't know why I should tell you all this, but ever since Deborah was a kid, I've had a sort of nose for trouble where she's concerned. The times I've got her out of jams by pure radar, and now it's working overtime again. You seem very interested, Miss Rayner. Why? If you know anything about her, or think you do, you really must tell me."

He was sharper than he seemed. I warmed towards

him, though I thought him heavy-footed and needed to know more.

"It's always possible she listens to her guardian by way of excuse. If you know someone very well, you still like to look round before you settle down. Make sure love isn't habit. It could be that you rushed her overmuch." I thought of Catherine's comments.

"Of course I did. I had to. Do you think I *wanted* actually to propose to anyone when I was in no position to take on a wife? It was just that competition was getting too darn hot and Deb was looking miserable and harassed. Lavinia would make a louse look virtuous, and her friends have the morals of tomcats. Deb'd be far happier living with my mother, as I told her. I said we could be married whenever she liked. You'd have thought that I'd insulted her. She went off in a rage. When I was taken ill, she didn't even visit me. Instead she rushed off somewhere while I was safely out the way. It's so stupid. She treats me as she ought to treat the others. She knows I only want to look after her. London gets worse and worse for girls."

Dangers were not confined to London, I thought wryly. The more he spoke, the less I thought him suitable to tilt with Peter. In a free fight he'd have my money, but in a straight romantic set he lacked finesse.

"No wonder that she ran away," I smiled. "You sound most prosaic."

He blushed again. "I mean what I say, at least, and she might be glad of it."

James shook with silent laughter. "Dear me, young man, you have the hero's cut. I'm sure that you'll slay dragons, armed with a set of blinkers. Alice can tell you

all about the visitors in Stranach. She stayed in the hotel
a day or two ago. Any stray golden girls at Mrs. Morrison's?"

I could have wrung his neck. No alternative but a half-
truth. "There aren't many young people," I said. "One
girl, as far as I remember, but she was with a friend and
pretty busy. I travelled in the train with this one."

"What does she look like?" asked David categorically.

"Oh, fairish, medium height, good legs, a nice com-
plexion. Quite pretty, but she wouldn't set the world on
fire."

"Man or woman?" he asked sharply. "I mean, the
friend you mention."

"A young man," I replied regretfully. "A mere fellow-
guest."

"I'd better take a look at them. Be on the safe side."

I was alarmed. "But David—may I call you that?
Supposing, just supposing, this was the girl? Though I'm
sure she doesn't use the name of Mansfield. Would she be
pleased to see you? Might she not resent your turning
up? She's enjoying life; taking a deliberate rest from all
her problems. You'd have to be most tactful."

"Naturally," said David grandly. "What name does she
use?"

I gave up. "Marston, I think—something like that.
You could, of course, pretend you landed here by accident. Certainly, if you did check, you should contrive to
see her alone and not embarrass her."

"I'm perfectly capable of handling my own affairs—
and Deborah's," he said coolly.

I wished for equal faith, but it eluded me.

Soon afterwards he took his leave, after a few more

vague literary overtures. James gave him even less encouragement and speeded him implacably.

"My dear Alice! Alone at last! So tell me what's your game. I note that Lochinvars come out of Whitehall nowadays, but really, need you matchmake for them? For I presume the millionairess is in Stranach. You looked abominably guilty."

"Would he have the same impression?"

"Oh, he grinds exceeding small, I imagine. But the plot, Alice, the plot! It sounds most antiquated and well worn, but pastiche is an art like any other."

He laughed like a hyena when I enlightened him, thinking it madly funny.

"You will prove useful, Alice, if I ever come to prostitute my writing. Though we may have trouble with verisimilitude."

"James, this is happening here and now, and hurting people."

"Which makes it fact, but not truth surely?"

"Truth! Are people ever honest with themselves? That girl is weaving herself a fiction as surely as you do, James, with your pen. What worries me is it's the sort of tale which ought to have a happy ending—but damned if I know how."

"You will arrange it, Alice, I am sure. I now see that you have unexpected lights beneath your bushel."

"I wonder what David will do."

"Probably take his second-fifteen frame to Mrs. Morrison's and murder off the rival. This will add a dash of something to your fiction—reader appeal perhaps."

"We haven't the same sense of humour."

"My dear Alice, you take it all too seriously. I suppose

the Hindemith is finished. Shall we have the talk on Brecht?"

"You can. I'm going for a walk. It might, who knows, assist my mental processes."

And I left him to the mercies of the Third Programme.


I'd shaken off my sense of pilgrimage. All places were alike to me. Apart from keeping clear of Castle Rannoch, I walked without direction, vaguely annoyed that Deborah's case should still claim me when my own concerns had loosened my hold. I took her back to heart reluctantly.

It was a very quiet night, scarcely a breath of wind. The moon was just perceptibly below the full, and the forest ride became a silver ribbon. Even the pines were silent, and halfway up the hill waves were still audible along the shore.

Deborah receded. More appropriate to think of Alastair, who belonged to this moon until its last expiry. Why not? It was deeply pleasant to remember, and surely no great harm in it—no harm at all.

"You walk late, mistress." I was pulled up sharply out of reverie, and a squat gnarled figure stepped out of the trees to bar my path. I once asked Nurse if Angus belonged to the Wee People. He was mischievous, alert, and old as all my time.

"Good evening," I said formally to gain my breath.

He stood his ground and adjusted a shotgun to his greater comfort.

"And what are you about?" he enquired.

"It was too glorious a night to stay indoors," I offered in keen, southern tones.

"Do you not know that this is Rannoch land?"

"Indeed? Does it matter? I know Mr. Forres slightly. I'm sure he wouldn't mind."

"These are Rannoch trees, and while I live I will see they come to no harm."

"I can assure you I'll not damage them."

"You'll be the London lady, I am thinking, who type-writes for yon author body. Do I not know the ways of such as you, who smoke like Jezebels and in the forest too?"

"Jezebel didn't smoke," I retaliated. "She had her vices, but that was not one of them. As for me, I have neither cigarettes nor matches with me. I wonder if you can say the same. And now, perhaps, you'll allow me to pass."

He did not move, except to put his gun at the ready.

"I am surprised, indeed I am, that the fat gentleman did not warn you how we treat the foreigners at Castle Rannoch."

"Do you intend to shoot me?"

"I am telling you to turn back, mistress, or it will be the worse for you."

"Well, you can save your breath, Mr. McDhui. I am going to the top to see the view. Put down that toy, and don't make a fool of yourself. I may come from London, but that's no excuse to shoot me at close range. How dare you threaten me?"

Such temerity, it seemed, was impressive. He more or less obeyed me, though not quite. He had aged consid-erably, Angus, and shrunk, as old men do. This I saw very clearly as he stepped forward and laid a wrinkled hand upon my arm.

"Are you not feart to walk alone, London woman?

There are strange things in the woods and forests of Glenshael, and those who watch and listen here are not of human kind. Have I not seen them when the moon is high, keening and greeting for the proud days behind them and the lost glory of their blood?"

"The Glenshael ghosts? I've heard about them."

"I am warning you. I am preparing you for what must come, if you walk alone tonight on Rannoch soil, and they waiting to strike down the ungodly."

"Ungodly? Aren't you rather sweeping?"

"I have myself been in the town of London, and a terrible place it is for sure, with its wild noise, and the smell of the pit, and the wickedness of yon folk who have the devil for their laird. My lost people do not want you here. It is better I should tell you, while there is still time, and the anger is not come upon you."

I whistled softly. Obstinate old fiend! So this was how he worked!

"I've a mind to report you to Mr. Forres. He knows that you tell ghost stories but not, I think, the lengths to which you go."

"As you will, mistress. Why would I be caring? I serve the Rannochs of Glenshael. I have known strangers come and go, and this one will follow, I am thinking. There is no mercy for those who take the Rannoch place. For the curse of the house is upon him."

"So you ill-wish him, do you?" I said softly.

"Did I say so? I cannot stop the dead from their task."

I was deeply shocked, and my anger had been growing steadily. I found it irrelevant to wonder if he was mad or bad. To tell the truth, I hardly cared.

"You ill-wish him," I repeated. "I know fine now who's

ungodly. The devil is behind you, I'm thinking. I'd not have your conscience for the world. And what is more, you dare to do it in the Rannoch name. Are you Glenshael yourself? Aye, and if you were, you would not talk such foolishness. The wind off the hills, the music of the Shael, these are the Rannoch heritage and need none of your protection. I'll tell you this, you'll stop this blether, Angus, for it is wickedness. Make no mistake. And I will not be having it."

"Aillie!" He muttered, half-bemused.

"Glenshael," I corrected haughtily.

"Is it yourself, my ain wee mistress? Is it yourself, returned to me at last?"

"Aye, to find myself a laughingstock for tourists. Are you sure I'm not one of yon keening ghosts? Where are they now, your lost ones? They can greet forever, but they can't alter facts. Mr. Forres owns their land and tends it well. He is a decent man and far too patient with a blethering old liar like yourself. Could he not have turned you out the house where you were born? Do you take bread from his hands and then ill-wish him? I'm thinking you are worse than Wise Janet. Are you not shamed?"

"Ach, but Aillie . . ."

"You'd best be careful the curse does not fall on you, for it is you who use my name and place."

"I thought you were the London lady. . . ."

"And so I am. Is that excuse for threats and mischief? What would my father say? I'm glad he is not here to see this day, but I must thole it. To meet again one I have loved well, and only see the blackness of his heart."

"I am an old man, Aillie, who has only lived to see your face again."

"And did not even recognize it!"

"It is a dark night."

"Nonsense! It's clear as day."

"My eyes are dim, Glenshael, and my hearing none so good."

"You're an old liar. Were you not always so? Aye, you're dim-eyed enough when you don't want to see. If you're so blind, and it's so dark—what about that gun? I'm thinking you're a public danger to the tourists."

"Ach, I can see all right, as well you know, but it's been ten years, Aillie, and you're changed. I do not think anyone would have known you."

"I did not wish them to."

"But you did not come to old Angus—could you not trust me? Would I ever cause you harm or sorrow, I who have saved you often from sore trouble, when the black mood was upon himself and the drink in him? I have served you, Aillie, since the day that you were born. I would do always what you say, if I had orders. But I waited for them, these ten years, and you silent."

"You can have some orders here and now, Angus. You will behave yourself from this time on. You can stop frightening folk with silly stories, or peppering poor Mr. Bywater with shot. And as for Mr. Forres, he's your employer and you owe him decency. I would like Glenshael to have a good name and the old evils forgotten. I can't mend what I did before I left. It's haunted me these many years. When I believed the thing half-cured, I come home to new mischief. It must stop, Angus. This alone is left of all my birthright, the power to dictate to you, and that only because you give it me with great generosity."

"It will be different now you're back, Aillie."

"But I can't stay, Angus *beag*. It's no longer my home. The foxes have their holes, but not Aillie Rannoch. Only my love remains, and that I can take with me everywhere I go, with the loyalty of my oldest friend and the moon above the pines."

"Are you wed, Aillie? You're all of twenty-six."

"Old and staid but very much a spinster, and a London woman, as you said. Remember how you used to tell me that the streets were paved with gold. You were right. But it's fairy gold, Angus, I am thinking."

"Aye, I was there to look for you—three weeks I stayed, a dreadful place indeed. I saw such things that I was frightened for you, but I knew fine you'd be there, if only I could find you."

"I'd have been very glad to see you, Angus, and I am touched that you sought me, but it was better we did not meet. The break had to be clean. In a way I'm sorry we've met here, though I am blithe to see you. It will make homesickness worse when I leave you once again."

"There would be others glad to know you were alive."

"I wonder. They were quick to bury me, I'm thinking. Nor have I any wish for resurrection. We'll leave well alone, Angus. Keep your mouth shut, so I can go as I have come, this time in peace. I'll not lose touch, I promise. But remember, you're the only one who knows, and let it rest there."

"I shall not betray you, my wee mistress."

"You haven't changed, my Angus. I keep remembering such silly things about the old days—wee incidents with

Morag, Nurse, and Miss Lamont. It's so changed. It's like a sort of jigsaw puzzle sometimes. So much remains, if you can find it, but the pattern is quite different."

The old man scratched his head, the way he used to do when I thought out loud.

"Ach, do ye still find life a toy, Allie? 'Tis time that you were wiser."

"I have my moments. For instance, it must be getting late and time that I went back. No, don't come down with me. We'd better not be seen together."

"But we'll have a longer crack together?"

"Of course. We'll meet in the old places till I go and no one but ourselves knowing."

"As ye will, mistress."

"As I will. There speaks a highland chief and her McDhui. Lord! I am out of practice and better stay so. We're feudal, Angus. Did you know? But it's fine to be myself, for all that."

# 13

## The New-Rigged Ship

I WOKE WITH a feeling of reprieve. There had never been a good reason for not seeing Angus, I had merely jibbed at the final bridging of the chasm between past and present. But now, at last, I had been recognized and felt the better for it. When I pulled back the heavy curtains, I viewed the new day without guilt. Lucky Angus to be out with his gun, concerned with dangers to the young birds. More my thing really than to type out deathly prose. It reminded me of going to school on summer mornings with envy and rebellion in my heart.

James was too niggling for my mood. I worked on automatically, my thoughts ranging. It was good to be called Aillie once again—and comforting to have an individuality. In a saner world, I'd live with Angus in his wee shieling, and have his porridge ready in the morning, and the peats glowing when he came home at night.

We spent all morning on six pages and tore them up before lunch. James seemed to imply that it was all my fault and in the afternoon set out for a solitary walk along the cliffs.

Soon after he had left, Catherine rang, and my heart sank at her first words.

"Panic all round. The you-know-whos have checked out. Apparently they went off very early, leaving no rack behind."

"I might have known," I muttered.

"I'm worried stiff. I feel responsible for her."

"It's not your fault; it's mine."

"I bet he tricked her in some way. She was telephoned late last night, the hotel said, after which no one saw her till they drove away. He had it all organized. He spread the news that there was illness in her family, and on no account was she to be disturbed, and they must leave first thing, and so on. No doubt he did it well. But, as we know, she hasn't got a family, and the operator thought the call was local before he undeceived her. I don't like the feel of it, Miss Rayner. Either he faked the call or cooked up some press alarm perhaps. It has to be to suit his own schemes."

"It's easier than that, I'm afraid. The alarm is likely to be genuine, and I don't like her reaction. There's a new member of the cast by the name of David Gregory. I should have let you know before but I've been nosing at the grindstone up till now." From now on it scarcely mattered if the calls were monitored, for Stranach would be talking anyway.

I therefore gave a full account of David, who must presumably have phoned after he left us. Warning with-

out restraining presence. Of all the damn-fool things to
do!

"Now we've lost all this time while the trail was fresh.
We have to find them without a clue."

"There's nothing we can do. They might be anywhere
by now."

"At least we can make some enquiries. We have their
car number. For instance, Robin's at the Kyle today and
he'll check up round there. Robin's as annoyed as I am.
He has some responsibility in his position. But the point
is, you are involved too, and we can't afford to ignore a
useful helper. We've no books here on the Scottish marriage laws. If Mr. Bywater hasn't either, there's a massive
library at Castle Rannoch. Would you find out about
domicile, and pick Alastair's brains at the same time?
You can delegate to him the checking of hotels around
Glenshael."

She sounded like a schoolmistress, and we parted stiffly.
I could work up no enthusiasm for the chase. Just the
same, I thought I'd better see Alastair, in case he felt we
ought to tell her guardians.

For the first time, I marched up to the front door of the
castle and rang the bell just like a proper caller. The
game stopped, though, when I was hailed by Alastair,
who was crossing the lawn to meet me. While I went
towards him, I noted he was wearing gum boots, slacks,
and guernsey, very open-air; and as we drew close, I
laughed outright. He had a glorious streak of mud across
his face.

"You're the very person I wished to see. I would have
waited till tomorrow, but as you've turned up, come down
to the pool. I have something to show you."

"Don't tell me one of your Amazons has actually flowered."

"I've a new species which I hope will do so."

"I can see you hope to reform me."

"I do, yes. Now close your eyes."

"What on earth for?"

"Because I say so, love. Do what you're told for once, and no questions. You see we've reached the river path. I'm now going to propel you."

I obeyed because I was intrigued, taking his arm and blindly staggering. I felt the flagged path and the incline, till I must have reached the place where we first met.

He appeared to place me at some vantage point, then stood behind me, arms about my waist.

"Now you can look," he said softly, "and tell me what you see."

Look! I gazed, I gasped. Below me was the Shael in spate. It writhed, it foamed, it swirled along its banks.

The river had gone free!

"It's so beautiful!" I said. And meant it. The dam had gone; the sickly plants removed. The smear of sludge, where the old dead pool had been, would soon dry out and grow soft turf, so a child could play there in the summer sun. Down came the last fall from the upper glen, no longer to be trapped and tamed. The water flicked away from it in reel-time and danced down to the sea.

"It's a bonnie stream, the Shael." I choked.

"Aye, love. It is for sure."

"What happened, Alastair? I don't understand."

"You can build a dam and also blow it up."

"But why? Weren't all your plants ruined?"

"I thought I'd be a public benefactor to the salmon.

Look! There's a flash already—in this water too. Does your heart leap up to see it?"

"I suppose you've decided to fish again. I heard you say you might at Ilsafeccan. But never mind about the motive—this is fact, and the Shael, I think, is grateful."

"You are a child of nature. You are retarded, and it's high time you grew up. You remind me of the princess and the spindle. Did you prick your finger sometime and go to sleep? One must hack back undergrowth certainly to wake you up."

"I doubt if you should play Prince Charming, Alastair. With that mud on your face, you are far more like a goose boy."

"Nevertheless," he answered in his most clipped voice, "you know the certain cure for sleeping beauties."

Not that I saw much point in waking up, but I owed him too much pleasure to refuse. Besides, there was a spell on me in this place where a girl had dreamed of life ahead. The glen, the Shael, and Alastair—strong medicine. I was awake indeed.

It was not until we went back to the house that I remembered Deborah, and told Alastair she'd gone.

"I was sent here today by Catherine to study tomes on law, though I doubt if I'll make head or tail of them."

"You needn't worry. I looked up Scottish marriage laws the other night, jotting down all the salient points. It would certainly be easier if they didn't cross the Border. I'll show you over tea. Go and sit down by the fire. I'd better wash, after all your rude remarks about my face."

Craigie was back in residence, a sober man with a long hatchet face. He brought in tea before I could protest,

and eyed me disapprovingly. I was glad when Alastair
came to the rescue and dire prophecies about the weather
ended.

Over several slices of buttered toast and honey, I re-
ported on all new developments, in exchange for a lecture
about domicile. "But all it adds up to is stalemate," I
concluded. "The Macdonalds of Anacher may be in full
cry, but Peter Rannoch is a wily fox. I doubt if anyone
can do anything, and frankly I don't care."

"You've changed your tune."

"Why not? They might be anywhere in Scotland—in a
back room in Glasgow Gorbals, second floor. I have a job
of work, as I told Catherine."

"Yet Rannoch's charms might well be reduced by
dingy town surroundings. He's gambled, after all, on clan
glamour. Don't you think he'd retain it as long as possible?"

"There's a lot of ground to cover and no idea where to
start. What I might try is to tell the boyhood sweetheart
the whole story. I suppose, like Catherine, you think I
should have told him *all* last night."

"You should have kept your mouth shut altogether.
You say he's a nice boy?"

"Nice is the word. And too self-confident. Because he's
known her all her life, he thinks he owns her, and the fact
she's turned him down and run out on him makes no
material difference."

"One sees his point of view," said Alastair, a trifle
reminiscently. "Good luck to him."

"He'll need it. She has all the wrong reactions. As far as
we can guess, he telephoned, she panicked, and then
turned to Peter. Not to the chap who helped her down

from apple trees. She's chosen the wrong man. A pity, but she's free and white, though rather underage."

"I wonder. I doubt if she was consulted. Rannoch was on the spot and worked on her. You admit she is infatuated, and he knows the ropes. Incidentally, he may not wait till marriage now, and your worst fears will be realized."

"You don't have much faith in her morals."

"Neither have you. So that makes two of us."

"All right. We ought to do something. But what I hardly know. The only thing which strikes me—it's a slender hope. Even David says that she's been building up to this highland holiday. She might be stubborn at having it curtailed. She must be spoilt, you know, and used to her own way, and she can't, after all, *fear* David. She wants to save herself embarrassment, perhaps publicity, but no need for her to fly the country and she'll know it."

"What interests me, they haven't turned up here. You'd think he'd show her the ancestral home. I assumed he would, and hotted up policing, but my spies report no sign of them."

"You mean he could be leaving it, and it's conceivable they may yet come?"

"As a preface to the final throw. I think it's possible."

"Good Lord! What to do then? Play cowboys and Indians in the glen? Over to you, Alastair. It's not my line of country. Besides, it's time I went back to James."

"I can't imagine how you stand that man."

"I do so admirably. I'm fond of James."

"So I have noticed."

"You would perhaps prefer him to be horrible. But it

wouldn't be much fun for me. He's nice and calculable, James. Better than you, who change each time I meet you."

"When I keep incalculable company."

"You don't have to, that's for sure."

"I am out of favour. Why is that? When I've loosed the Shael entirely for your pleasure."

"I doubt it."

"But indeed I did, nor was I disappointed. You lit up with diffused radiance. I'm still wondering why."

"Don't start up again, Alastair. And let me go. Anyone might see us through the window."

"Who cares? They have to know sometime. We can't go on like this indefinitely."

"Know what? That I consult a book and stay to tea? Is that so strange? Are you so far from general life and custom that you make mountains out of molehills?"

"Do I? Are you sure, my love?"

"Of course!" I panicked. "Do you take me seriously? I don't see why you should at all. I've kissed hundreds of men. Once started, it seems quite the thing to do. But not here, Alastair, I daren't be the butt of village gossip, or I daresay a mild flirtation might prove most amusing, for there's not so much selection in a place like this."

"So now I know." He winced at such cheapness. I didn't blame him.

"A middle-aged Lothario," I added for good measure. No point in leaving him with sentimental memories. "To my mind, you're as slick as Peter Rannoch, but I'm no Deborah Mansfield."

As he was silent, it was difficult to push back tears. My desperation needed more outlet. I acted well, I think, but words tripped me up. I had to go on talking to fill the vacuum.

"I suppose you want more payment for the Shael—you judged my price well. But not well enough, Mr. Forres. For I'm not on the market. I go free too—my pride with me."

He looked exceedingly bewildered. I didn't trust myself to stay with him, instead I nearly ran. I didn't even try to say goodbye. I couldn't.

All down the lower glen I saw his face, while that daft river laughed at its new freedom. It filled its banks, spilt into pools of flood water; it leapt the boulders, foamed into the troughs.

What else could I have done? What else? With Alastair assuming far too much. No half measures at all, not either way. Break clean, no point in crippling. A prize bitch—well, I'd lived up to the title. He was used to decent women, Alastair.

"You'll have been up at the house, I am thinking."

"God, Angus! You made me jump! Yes, I have. I was borrowing a book."

"And having tea, my niece Elspet said."

"Tea too. What's so extraordinary in that?"

"Only that Mr. Forres has changed colour like a mountain hare. He's not so fond of ladies' company as a rule. It is in my mind, Aillie, you could do worse than that. He has plenty money, I am told."

"Ach, you think so? Well, you can think again. You run ahead too fast."

" 'Tis a pity his father was from the east coast, and he was bred in that place, London. But happen you would not be minding that, being so full of it yourself. He told me once his mother came from Fort John, and he was born there in the hospital."

"What's that to do with it?"

"He's partly highland and takes after the Fort John Mathesons. They are only crofting people, I have heard, but folk aren't so particular these days."

"Forget it," I said curtly. Trust Angus to examine pedigrees.

"Now Aillie, it would be a fine thing. I've been thinking, you are twenty-six. It's high time you were wed. There's a foolishness in putting off the bairns. You know what happened to your mother in her thirties. The sooner you get on with it, the better, and we needing heirs of Rannoch blood."

"Angus McDhui!" I exploded. "Will you stop your blether, please! Can I not drink a cup of tea with Mr. Forres without you hatching out a clutch of weans?"

"Would you wish that some Americans took over? It aye worried himself, as well you know. It is your duty, Aillie, to your family, and I the only one who's left to tell you so. This Mr. Forres may not be much, but owning Castle Rannoch makes him suitable. You could fare far worse, and get back your own place, and bide among us."

"You've been thinking overtime."

"I think ye have a good chance. The rich men often like a wife from the old families. I don't say that he'd be an easy fish to catch, or that you'd be the first to make a cast, but you've made a start and I can help. We can take him together."

"So now I sell myself for Rannoch land—am bought up like a brood mare? Fine stock for sure! I'm not much of a bargain. My precious line is not worth the trade. Think of

it, Angus—rakes and spendthrifts, murderers, thugs, and
even suicides. It's wild blood, Angus; not many would
want it. Before I cursed myself, they'd all cursed me."

"Is that what frets you, Aillie? Why you have stayed
single?"

"I don't know, Angus. I don't know. Why does one fall
in love? Why does one *not?* But I'll not be stalking a rich
husband anyway. I would think shame to do it. What's
money? Once, not so long ago, I had enough to buy back
Castle Rannoch, if I would. It was too late then, and it's
later now. I'll dree my weird."

"As you say, mistress, but it's daft talk."

"I'll tell you if I change my mind and start a new clan
in the outer suburbs. But I've burnt my boats meanwhile."

"You are unhappy, Aillie."

"It will not be the first time, Angus, or the last."

I left him, my thoughts more jumbled than before.
How much truth had I spoken? My outburst had surprised me. It reminded me of someone I hadn't recon-
sidered, a confused girl in London, facing not only loss of
material heritage but the illusions and the pride as well.
Father had killed himself. Way back, the excuse of feuds
would often cover murder. Scandal of some sort went
with Rannochs. They weren't exactly normal.

No doubt I had been too extreme. A more healthy
attitude came with new interests and hard work. Had it
gone into subconscious storage and caused my flippancy
towards marriage? Joe had a family by his former wife.
There was no problem there.

The excuses for my weird nobility were totting up.
Another thing. Supposing we forgot first wives, and Ran-

noch blood, and decency. Without such impediments, Angus had shown an utterly new picture. The irony! They'd all say I'd come back to trap Alastair. And do it to regain my acres! You could imagine sly congratulations. The odd thing was, I'd never thought of it. Secret return, discreet liaison, and hook my pretty fish. Moreover, Alastair might think so too if he knew my real identity. For some reason, this wasn't tolerable. No wonder I had clutched at every straw.

I must get out of this mess at once. So far so good, but I had poor stamina. My grip was loosening. I made mistakes. I'd soon betray myself.

No, it was necessary to go into new exile.

# 14

## Meg Merrilies

I WAS RESTLESS. The freedom of the Shael infected me. A mood I might have stilled with work but James returned with blisters and exhaustion, and preferred domesticity.

My knitting looked more hideous than usual. I was sick and tired of "dear Alice," who hugged the fireside like a cosy cat instead of hunting in the waking night.

"Damn!" I exclaimed at each stitch dropped. Nurse would have sniffed at both my language and my handiwork.

"This place is demoralizing," James grumbled in his turn. "I cannot imagine why I chose to climb Beinn Cullach. It's a dull bare spot, inhabited by nasty predatory birds. How I detest Nature. I have, at times, enjoyed the Pyrenees, but why these ugly humps are called mountains . . ."

"But they're not," I interrupted tartly. "They are *hills* to any real Scot. If the southron wishes to name them otherwise, that is no fault of ours. As for the Pyrenees, you're welcome to them."

"One sees exactly," he ignored me, intent on his own line, "why the painter wings south like a swallow, towards clear vivid light and cardinal colours. It's been a perfectly fine afternoon, yet all these celebrated views were wrapped in muting haze."

"I often wonder why you live here, James, for nothing in the highlands suits you. I bet you'd be far happier reprinting the footsteps of Cézanne, or trudging naked on your pavements."

"I cannot expect the philistine to comprehend the importance of creative frustrations. Detachment is necessary to sublimate the object of care. Contrast distills essentials."

"Nonsense," I retorted, in no mood for his higher flights of rhetoric. "Detachment is inherent, not topographical."

"But my dear Alice, I disagree. Now I write about industrial towns, and from here I see their shape and colour clearly. I write about real people and their dilemmas, safely stowed myself amid stylized romantics. I was born and reared in an ugly Midland town where nothing thrived, not even wickedness. My background was a decaying terrace house, not only hideous but scarcely sanitary."

"But your home. It must have stood for something?"

"For tedium and frustration."

"And the people—your parents?"

"Were worthy, respectable, and uninspiring. My father was a gas fitter."

"What's that to do with how you felt about him?"

"I suppose in puking infancy there were reflex affections; if so, they left no record except guilt. My strongest, most enduring emotion was the will to escape my ridiculous environment and acquire new horizons. My brain was good enough by Board School standards, and I learnt that I could use it constructively to gain my ends."

"And write about the setup left behind you? Have you escaped, in fact? We're bound inexorably; a penalty we pay. Our backgrounds mean too much, too early. A pity to regard them, then, with neither warmth nor understanding. Hampering, even crippling. You might, James, have become a happy gas fitter; and Bunyan was a tinker, wasn't he?"

"Laugh on! I know it's humorous—which is why I seldom mention my beginnings."

"It's not funny; it's pathetic. You English are such shocking snobs. No Scot would call his father *worthy* with a sneer. You're actually ashamed he fitted gas, which is a very useful thing to do. You should be proud he was respectable. Mine wasn't, I can tell you. He drank himself to decadence; he was a terror with the women; and in debt to everyone for miles around. Yet if he had been twice as bad, it would have made no difference. I would have loved him just the same; I'd miss him, as I miss him to this day. Go on about yourself."

"Little enough to tell. I went up to Cambridge on a scholarship and learnt that I was second rate. I then taught at a loathsome school. I wrote an unsuccessful masterpiece and had to go on teaching."

"Quite wrong. You should have starved in a garret."

"It would have been a trifle hard on my wife."

Her introduction gave me no particular surprise. The

bachelors in this neighbourhood appeared to run to pattern.

"Wife? Is she still alive?" I enquired to keep things straight.

"Good Lord, yes! Why, did you think I'd murdered her? I know your hankering for the outré. She lectures in classics at a red-brick university. We're divorced now, heaven be praised! Though I still receive a Holy Family reproduction every Christmas."

"What a pity it broke up."

"A merciful release, my dear Alice. I married, as you would expect, above my station—a fellow undergraduate of upper-class extraction. You must know, she had faith in me. It dogged me, morning, noon, and night. She aimed to be the inspiration of my genius, till the influence grew so pervasive I ceased to write at all. You asked why I live here. Answer: Charlotte. Divorce and desertion weren't enough. It needed several hundred miles of poor communications to escape her friendly influence. She's too noble to bear malice, my dear wife."

"If any man deserted me, I'd cut his throat."

"But you, as one now sees, are scarcely civilized. A calm exterior suppresses violence and passion. Moreover, you are capable of wanton interference on a far grander scale than my discarded mate."

"Men always feel their psyches threatened," I said cheerfully. "It shows how little that they have to lose." The present situation on the whole did not displease me. If I came, in my turn, to bear the blame of ruined chapters, James would gladly speed the parting secretary and find someone more bolstering to his ego.

Or *I* would. I must give him real attention.

"Poor James!" I added far more kindly. "You've had more than enough nagging for today. I'm going for a walk."

I was still restless. I escaped with almost panther impetus. The moon stood at the full. It was the time when Aillie Rannoch walked. The black woods waited, the freed Shael expected her. They called, and knew that she would answer.

I did feel oddly spectral as I went through the village. My pale clothes were silvered by the light. The only creature stirring was a dog who bristled as I passed, as if unsure of my mortality. No wonder I'd felt caged and fey on this my scheduled night for exercise!

I dropped into the glen where the fencing had been battered down by children. I walked beside the Shael whose rough water broke the moonbeams into threads and spun them easily into magic. The secret people watched me go—the timid mice, the knowing owls, the otter from his holt. Behind each bush you thought to see the sly eyes and pointed ears of the Good Folk. The dead also? Who could know? However, on the tall slab of rock ahead, no old wife was dancing in her grave clothes. When I was small, I'd wait and wait in hopes one day of seeing her.

Some people did; or so they said. And mostly they saw me. Father had skelped me more than once for scaring lovers out of shotgun weddings. Not that I cared. I did no harm, and it was grand up there above the world. I used to feel triumphant, and indeed a thought immortal.

Now I obeyed an impulse to climb it once again, barefoot and childlike, gripping naked rock. Lord, I was stiff. These days I felt an old wife myself, and as usual the last clamber grazed my knee.

Fine to be back there, quite alone, nearer the stars, the water far below. It was a vantage point for sentries in the old fighting days, where you could see an enemy approach; though ten to one he would not notice you. All sounds were amplified by the surrounding rocks, so you could pitch an echo marvellously. It was just the sort of eerie place to prompt legends. I coughed. It bounced off like a chucky-stane and skimmed into the shadows.

I first learnt voice control on Margaret's Rock. I'd trip off speeches and the birds would fly away. I'd give an eldritch shriek to the echoes. Or I would whisper softly, very softly, and listen to it hover like a hawk.

I wondered if I dare try again. I almost did so; then I realized there were already voices in the glen. Footsteps too, which surely came towards me. Nearer and nearer . . . and with them recognition. That boyish tenor was familiar. Peter and Deborah! New trespassers for Alastair; and Angus sleeping on the job, it seemed.

Amazing! Had I the sight like Aunt Johann? Was this why I'd been called from my knitting? So he had come in the end to show his lady her inheritance. But what a time to choose! And what to do about it?

"We're coming up to Margaret's Rock." He was still on folklore. Was the girl insatiable? What a sad waste—a grand moon, a lonely glen, and mossy banks galore. Not my idea of high romance to dig up ancient history.

"I'm sure we oughtn't to be here, Peter." Deborah did not sound happy.

"You're shivering. Don't tell me that you're scared! Darling, it's just a tale."

"I don't like this place. Let's go back to the car. We're trespassing. You know we are. Supposing we are caught?"

"Then I'd tell this Forres man exactly what I think of him. I'd rather enjoy that, come to think of it. However, sweet, we're absolutely safe. You don't know country hours."

"It's wrong. And it feels wrong."

"It's dead right, darling. Seeing my Diana, my moon-goddess, in her own setting. This is your future home, my dearest. There's your moon. Diana's glen."

I thought him flowery. A maiden-goddess, was she? Well, others walked by moonlight in that place.

"Wrong," she repeated stubbornly. "Besides, there's a funny feel about this glen. As if something is listening, watching us. It's legendary but horrid. Yes, I *am* afraid."

"With me? With a Rannoch? Darling, you'll never make a chieftain's wife unless you're tougher. But it's a shame to tease you. You're safe with me, even from superstition. Keep close; don't spoil it for me. I've lived for this, my sweet."

I wondered how she stomached it, though he made a nice change from David. Still, there were indications she was wearing thin.

"I wish we'd stayed at Portneish for the dance. I've been bitten, and my feet are cold and wet."

She sounded thoroughly disgruntled.

Portneish! I might have known it. A big enough hotel to avoid attention, with all the inmates golf- or fishing-mad. The luck was running my way and no sign it was exhausted. For up till now their argument had kept them occupied, their eyes upon each other. I could have hit them with a pebble, but they had not seen me. The Fause

Rannoch . . . Mad Margaret. It was too good a chance
to miss. If I had caught young Aillie's reasoning, I'd
caught her mischief too. Why not? Why the hell not? If
anything, my acting had improved.

At this point, Peter gave up cajoling and proceeded to
disperse her ill-mood by another method. He clasped her
expertly and wasted not much time in kissing her. Yes, it
might soothe her qualms, for he was very Hollywood.
Still, the embrace was useful, allowing me to adjust my
would-be grave clothes and claw my wig to flying elf-
locks. The dappled light would help preserve the illusion.
If I couldn't get away with this, I wasn't Aillie, or indeed
Anna Rayner.

"Who walks so late?" I interrupted them with chilling
softness. "Who walks when the foxes keep their holes and
the sma' birds their nests? Who are ye, bold and blithe,
beside the Shael upon this night of nights, when the moon
is at the full and the water angry with the waste of
years?"

Deborah broke loose at once. "What was that?" she
cried.

"Well may ye ask, woman of the Sassenach. I am the
guardian of the Rannoch name."

"Peter—you must hear it too, you *must!* I believe it's
that woman who haunts . . . Oh, my God! Yes! Look!
There she is! I can *see* her. I knew this place was horrible; I knew!"

"Darling, don't panic. Keep a grip. It's probably some
silly hoax. Hey! You up there—on the rock! What the
hell do you think you're doing?"

When in doubt I prefer immobility to gestures, and
meanwhile I raised my voice to full pitch and threw it to
the echoes.

"Wae to ye! Wae to ye, man of the stranger! Wae to
ye, fause usurper! Can I not see the blackness of your
heart? Does it not grieve me sair to know what I must
do? It has been spoken—aye and written too—that I do
not spare those who claim my name. You travel forward,
stranger, to your end. The light is on my face, and the
darkness of death lies behind me. Look at me well. This
night have they called me from my cold grave to fulfill
the duty laid upon me, and the Shael is ready to receive
its new burden and its care."

"But he *is* called Rannoch—Peter Rannoch." Deborah,
to my surprise, was showing fight in her own way.

"Do you say so, pretty lady? Ach, but I know my own.
He is no Rannoch of Glenshael. There is a foolishness in
you to play with such a one. Would ye not grow old by
your hearthstane with the love of your ain kind? Can you
not see the lust for yellow gold in this man's eyes? It is
not love but greed he feels for you, and you so young and
silly in your ways."

"This is beyond a joke," Peter sneered in some attempt
perhaps to break the spell. In Deborah, however, I had
audience participation.

"Do the dead lie? What need have they? Truth is
beyond the grave. I will tell you, Englishwoman, that you
put the path of happiness behind you and plunge into the
murk of unknown things. Is it too late? I can see great
cities in far, foreign lands. . . . I can see a great house
with a marble stair. Are there not bonnie bairns who wait
their mother? And a fine man with an honest heart? You
have known him love you in your father's house. He has
watched over you these many years. Will you break so
true a heart, Englishwoman? Will you not love the laddie
with the yellow hair?"

"David!" She gasped and high time too. I couldn't keep this up much longer. Spae-wives are so appallingly verbose, one wondered how they managed.

"I am the dead. I am the living. I am the name of Rannoch. The bats may cling to the ruined walls of my house, the weeds may spring where I walked, but I remain, to lay my curse on the unrightful claimant and see the devil takes his own."

At which I laughed. I knew exactly how. In the old days I'd practiced tirelessly to trap that fiendish cackle, and now I brought it out in wild abandon. At the first wave, Deborah ran. She swallowed back a scream and shook off Peter's arm. I heard her footsteps stumbling over loose stones till the Shael obliterated them. It was a headlong flight of utter panic, and with it the act ended.

I was alone with Peter. The true, the false Glenshael. I'd have been glad of Margaret's company. This was the reckoning.

"Right! Now let's get this straight. Who are you? What's your game?"

I had forgotten people could speak through their teeth. It sounded menacing.

No answer naturally. I preferred to weigh him up. There was a swagger in his tone which hinted at uncertainty. Was that a help? Frightened dogs bite the worst. And this young cur meant business. I'd spoiled his schemes and made a fool of him. His first step was to call my bluff. His next . . . ? I felt an odd, uneasy respect for my namesake.

He studied me from several angles, then he made up his mind. Ghost or no, he'd play this out. He hesitated once or twice as he drew near the rock but, gathering new confidence, at last determined on the climb. Out of sight now. The means to climb the sheer face lay in shadow. He would find them certainly, but it would slow him. Meanwhile I must think quickly.

Ghosts, of course, melt to nothingness, but how could I? The bare rock offered no cover, the trees were out of reach. To drop down the river precipice and ape-hang there was now beyond my scope. An eldritch screech? A dive into the Shael? Enough water certainly to make it possible, but whereas a teenage truant might well have enjoyed it, I disliked both broken bones and pneumonia.

I made no headway. Peter did. His hands now gripped the ledge. Could I perhaps dislodge them, so he'd fall? But that would be equivalent to murder. All right for the old Rannochs not to jib at killing, but modern justice was rather more far-reaching and efficient. And Cousin Rannoch was not worth my hanging.

So far I was clear-headed, but this stopped when he gave one last pull and then stood upright. Fear, rage, and effort had combined to give his face a curious inhumanity. I wasn't used to quite such ugly customers, and I froze to a statue.

It was the best thing that I could have done. The slightest movement would have given him his cue, but as it was he couldn't be altogether sure. You saw this, in his shifty snarling look. Only a few feet of rock still divided us, but we remained apart.

I had not realized he was so much taller. Strongly built too, with flexing muscles. My throat was dry. Amazing to be so afraid. A female coward, aching for protection. Falling in love is apt to make folk spineless. In some extreme of misery, I groped towards Alastair. I needed him; he ought have been there; I was no longer anything without him. Peter moved at last—in an unexpected way. He circled round me like an animal, as if to test my nerve. This brought him right above the deeper water. Here was the chance to push him backwards; but the trouble was, I found I couldn't move. I was wholly paralyzed, the old nightmare effect, stuck to my plinth as surely as a statue. When he raised his hands almost to neck level, I could only give a little strangled cry.

At once there was a shot. I'm told that it was single, but the echoes turned it to a fusillade. The effects were multiple. It dislodged the biggest owl I'd ever seen, a great bird with glowing yellow eyes who swooped towards the rock with a wild cry. The eldritch screech! But it was Peter who plunged into the Shael, shouting out too, as he mistook his footing and fell back in the pool. Myself I tried a hesitant scream too, but it turned into a laugh far worse than Mad Margaret's. For the first time in my life, I had hysterics, and it wasn't the best place.

My mind told me that Peter must have been killed outright, which seemed irrelevant at that moment. I was more intent upon the bird, which returned, nearly to touch me with its wings. And that was how I moved at last, to escape what seemed the vengeance of the dead; and the trouble was, once started all was panic. I don't remember getting down the rock, only the bird above, circling and circling. Once on the ground I fought nausea. I felt awful, limp and ill. The air was full of noises—more things in heaven and earth—and I had mocked the spae-wife in my wickedness.

"Ach, there you are! What mischief is this, Aillie? Old as you are, you need a skelping, I am thinking. Who's yon fine gentleman you pushed in the water?"

"I did not; he fell because you shot him. We'll all be hanged, I'm thinking, for the ill-luck's come upon us for our evil ways."

"What wild talk's this? Get yourself up from yon damp moss and use some sense. You're a grown woman, not a greeting bairn."

"I feel sick, Angus."

"And serve you right. Best get it over, or get over it. I need a hand."

"Did you see the great bird with the awful eyes—a dead soul flying, Angus?"

"Ach, what blether! Birds, is it? This glen has never lacked them, I am thinking, and the poor beasts disturbed with all the noise. I thought you had got over such silly fright, but I mind you never did like the big owls when you were wee."

"Did you shoot him dead or was he drowned?"

"The gentleman? Ach, neither. Do you think I'd be so daft as to hit him, and you two close together? It was a warning just. As for drowning, I myself pulled him up onto the shingle. Terrible cold the water was—I'll suffer for it, come the morn, you'll see."

"And he's all right?" I gasped stupidly.

"A wee thought unconscious, but ach! nothing serious, but we'll have him up the bank just the same, and you can lend a hand. You can croon o'er him to your heart's content when he's on dry land."

"He was out to do me mischief. He looked like murder."

"Because you sent the young woman away?"

"How long have you been here? Aye, just that. And moreover, Angus, he calls himself Rannoch of Glenshael, the creature, so I gave him the traditional treatment. I scared her, but he kept his head. You saw what happened."

"Glenshael? Is it possible? Ach, you did right then, Aillie. I thought you might have wanted him yourself, or I'd have made a small diversion earlier."

"I wish to heaven you had. But let's take a look at him to see what harm's been done."

"Glenshael! I should have let him drown," the old man muttered.

But I was feeling better.

Peter was lying in the shallows with his head upon the bank. He was unconscious, white as lard, and bleeding from some cuts. Angus informed me, not without real glee, these were due to rough handling and wholly superficial.

"And as for bones, I have run over him and find nothing amiss. I do not think we need be gentle to him. You take one shoulder. I will take the other."

No sooner had we placed him on the path than Angus handed me his gun and started to truss Peter like a hen.

"We'll take no risks. An old man and a weak lassie. He'll be round soon, and making trouble."

"I think we ought to get him to the house. He looks ghastly, Angus. Could we manage him together, do you think? Or shall I run for help?"

"The walk will do him good—restore the circulation—and a shotgun in the back will keep him fine and warm. Ach, the effrontery of the creature! We'll pay him back, I think, a wee bit more."

"Even so, I'd better warn Mr. Forres."

"You will do no such thing! We'll keep you out of this entirely. Would you wish all the neighbourhood to know about such ploys? Playing ghosts when decent folk are in their beds—alone and fooling with a man like this—and as for calling on a bachelor at such an hour, I never heard the like. You're a grown woman, Aillie Rannoch, and must learn seemly ways."

"Even so, Angus . . ."

"Will you be ever arguing? As ye ken fine, it would be foolishness. Have you not said yourself you would avoid the gossip? I will explain these things in my own way, and you have not been in the glen tonight, I'm thinking. As for this bit body here, it's likely he will doubt the morn that ye were flesh and blood."

"I hope you're right. It sounds sense anyway." I knew I could trust Angus to cope ingeniously with even the most improbable dilemmas. Meanwhile, I recollected, there was Deborah, and something must be done.

"Angus, you must keep this man out of my way for hours, if you can. I don't mind how you do it, fair means or foul, but nothing daft, mind. Another thing, the girl who came up with him. I'd like to keep her out of it as well."

"I will do all you say, mistress," said Angus in a lower tone, "but be still now, he is coming to himself. Hide in the bushes till I have him moving, and then away to your bed. I'll keep him occupied, you'll see, but stay out of more mischief yourself."

There was no time for further explanation, so I backed into the undergrowth discreetly. First Peter muttered something, then he sat up. No doubt his memory was still confused, and Angus opened fire before it straightened out.

"I have ye, aye and tied up fast, ye thieving Glesga

devil! Would ye poison the good water that was given us to drink? Would ye take the poor dead creatures from the river, ye born villain? Ach, that's a dirty city trick. It's terrible the wickedness of some folk."

"Where am I?" Peter asked with a groan.

"Where ye have no right to be—on private grounds. And to no good ends, that's clear. We'll see what the laird will say to this. A black time we have had with the poaching. I'm thinking he'll be blithe to see you, or myself I would have left ye there to drown."

"I'm no poacher."

"Did any man admit it ever? What else would you be doing?"

Still confused, Peter merely shook his head and looked more carefully about him. One could see details were coming back to him, for he looked up at Margaret's Rock, empty now but for my enemy, the screech-owl, who had settled there to check up on proceedings.

"I must have fallen in the river. . . ."

"That's certain, for I pulled you out myself, when your fine city friends had left you helpless, afraid of one old man alone."

"Friends? Christ! So I'm a member of a gang?"

"Just that, ye bold blasphemer. Did I not hear them with my own ears, yelling and arguing together?"

"I was alone—except . . ." He looked up to the rock again and hesitated. "Look here, my good man, you're totally mistaken. I'm sorry if I'm trespassing. I didn't realize. But I can assure you that my purpose was quite innocent."

"Aye, they all say something of the sort," said Angus.

"And waste their time and mine. Up wi' you now. It's time I took you to the castle. This gun is loaded. No tricks, mind, or you'll be fine and sorry."

He poked the shotgun amiably into the small of Peter's back, before he raised more protests. The false Rannoch was disconcerted and I saw him give the old man a narrowed, dangerous look. What he saw, however, did not reassure him, and he may well have decided Castle Rannoch preferable to death by an eccentric hand in a dark wood. At any rate, he did obey instructions, and as he walked ahead of Angus I noted with immense relief his movements showed no pain or injury, and if he had a headache—serve him right!

There was nothing more that I could usefully do, so I set off down the glen towards the bridge. Inspection of the roadside turf showed up a set of car tracks, fairly recent, that came and went towards the south. Young Deborah had not waited for her escort to return, and presumably had headed towards Portneish.

That she'd driven off and left him to his fate suggested she had finished with him. It was unlikely, then, she'd loiter in one place, so I must catch her up without delay. David. He had a car. I couldn't handle this alone. Besides, while she was half-hysterical and disillusioned, she'd pine for the familiar. It was an almost perfect opportunity for any boy-next-door.

For surely even David Gregory could scarcely bungle this. Though best I should be there myself to teach him elementary diplomacy. Fine thing to be a coach to Foreign Office hopefuls when what I really wanted was my bed.

I sighed, for there was no alternative to suit my conscience.

Like Ariel, I had always one more task ahead. I yawned—I always think of Shakespeare when I'm bothered. "Quickly, spirit, thou shalt ere long be free."

# 15

## The
## Caledonian Rant

To CHEAT IS human and I think less confusing.

To keep the right time sequence, I had best record what Angus told me, well edited, of course, for there was no end to the embellishments supplied for my private admiration. Angus could never hold the Sassenach was worthy of fair play; his delight was to cause every foreigner discomfort; and as for Peter, setting up in sacred office, there was even less excuse for mercy. The old man shook with silent laughter at the memory.

The Rannoch claimant did not look his best by strong electric light, and Craigie thought the worst of him without undue persuasion. He could not, however, thole such dripping objects on the good carpets, so produced a new outfit from items waiting for the next Jumble Sale. Thus Peter, who relied so much on clothing for effect, was put at disadvantage. His assorted wear was too big, or too small, and bore the creases of its bundling. He stood up to this first ill-usage well, and showed much resignation. No doubt he felt some small relief at being dry again.

"Ye may sit yourself on yon chair made of antlers." Angus, I'd guess, was grinning like a Cheshire cat to see his handiwork. Compassion for the wicked had never been his strong suit. He poked his victim with his gun again while Craigie swept the Monarch of the Glen gear away.

"Be still! I'll take no risks forbye. I know the ways you have in Glesga. Knives, broken bottles, and the like. It's all in the papers for decent folk to read."

"I happen to come from London, not from Glasgow."

"Is that a fact? From London they are coming, is it? Just for a fish or two! Who'd have believed that now?"

Craigie returned but either did not enter in the conversation or Angus did not think his comments worth recording.

" 'Twas bad enough with yon Colin McNichol, Mr. Craigie. But now I don't know what the world is coming to, I'm sure."

At this point Alastair came on the scene, severely dressing-gowned and with so thunderous an expression even the spritely Angus quailed.

"What is all this about, McDhui? Is it necessary to drag me up at this hour of night to see your captures? Do you know the time? God damn it, man! What is the police force for?"

"Ach, I am sorry, Mr. Forres; I am indeed. But I am an old and ignorant man, you see. I did not like to deal alone with gangsters from the city. This bold, wicked creature is from London, so he says. I had not thought things were as bad as that. I did my best, sir. Yes indeed. I know this one was all I caught, and others got away. But I was all alone and could not manage, though I held this one fast. He fell into the river and I saved his life. The Shael is wild in its new freedom. He'd have been drowned for sure, and no loss, I am thinking."

"Let's have this straight. I'm still half-asleep, so don't go round in circles. You caught him poaching? Is that it?"

"He did nothing of the sort," Peter now interrupted. "He does seem to have pulled me out the river, but no need to behave like a madman. I cannot get it in his addled head that I'm no poacher, there was no gang, and I am perfectly respectable."

Alastair looked him up and down and did not seem impressed.

"Then what were you doing on my land so late at night?"

"I was walking in the glen."

"You were trespassing then, and you admit it?"

"I suppose so. I was with a girl. She had a yen to see the place by moonlight. I'm afraid I humoured her."

"McDhui, was there any girl?"

"None that I saw, sir. Though you never know with such people. I have heard there are bad women in their gangs."

"Did you hear female voices?"

"No, sir. I did not."

"Then you must be bloody hard of hearing," Peter interposed. "For as it happened, I said very little. The females did all the talking between them. If you were in the neighbourhood at all, you couldn't miss them."

"Am I a liar?" Angus asked the ceiling. "Would I not

think it strange at once to hear womenfolk so late? And they feart of the bogles in the glen? Voices, I heard, I do admit, and saw people moving in the distance, but when I came to Margaret's Rock they were away. Except for this one in the big pool, where ye ken fine, sir, the great salmon rest. Unconscious he was, for five minutes or more. If he'd been with a lassie for the courting, would you not think she'd help? But now he says that there was more than one with him. Ach, but there's no believing what these folk will do."

Angus was always guaranteed to throw spanners by the handful. It was an old game, which had often stood me in good stead.

"Be quiet!" snapped Alastair. "When I need your views, McDhui, I will ask you. And meanwhile try to answer *yes* or *no.*"

"Yes, sir," muttered Angus meekly, "but I only do my duty, I am sure."

"Very well, young man. We'll have your name."

"Smith," said the erstwhile Rannoch very glibly. "Peter Smith, to be precise."

"Indeed? Not Jones or Brown?" Alastair sneered. It was, in fact, a silly blunder. He must have been too optimistic. Either he judged himself unrecognizable, or that escape was within his reach. And apparently he hadn't noted the outsiders in the train.

"Well, Smith, according to your statement, you went for a walk with one or two women, climbing my fences and ignoring notices. You loitered in my grounds though you were not poaching. One wonders why."

"I was with one girl, my fiancée. The reason's obvious."

"I fail to see why I should patronize your amatory

exploits. And where is this girl now? Why did McDhui not see her? And why did she leave you to drown?"

"Happen she pushed him in," suggested Angus. "He looks the sort who gives the lassies trouble. That would be self-defense, ye ken, and no exactly murder. Ach, it's terrible to think such things should be, and I so close I might have caught her, though I do not believe myself that she was there at all."

"I told you to be quiet," said Alastair. "Well, Smith, I'm waiting for a credible reply."

"The place was eerie—scared her—so she ran away."

"She evidently doesn't find you reassuring."

"She thought she saw a ghost. Why the hell not? Your blasted glen is haunted."

"She sounds a highly nervous individual. But you did not accompany this fiancée and console her?"

"I wished to investigate."

"Exactly what?"

"The ghost, of course. I thought it was a hoax. And somehow I fell into the Shael."

"A likely story! Angus pulled you out of mid-river, and anyhow the path is wide by Margaret's Rock. So how did you get into the pool, Mr. Smith? Unless you were already there for the black-fishing?"

"I don't know where I was. It's that man's word against mine. l just remember falling off the rock."

"The rock? And what the hell were you doing there?"

"He'll have been helping with the torches," Angus supplied with ingenuity. "I found a great one in his pocket. They have the electric kind these days."

"Something makes sense at last," said Alastair.

"Good God! I tell you, I'm a bona-fide tourist. I am a fisherman, but not on other people's water."

"Then why climb rocks and fall in salmon pools? Bona-fide indeed! You look a ruffian to me."

"Then I'm not the only one. How about him? He must have shot at me, if you really want to know. As I was pretty near the edge, I lost my footing."

"Ach, what will he say next?" demanded Angus. "That would be foolishness in me to give them all a warning. And would I not have heard a shot myself? No, if they wished him out the way, I'm thinking they'd have drowned him."

Peter had had a long unpleasant evening, and his temper was fraying.

"Christ! What a bunch! Can't any of you understand plain English. I was only with a girl. We saw a ghost. She ran away. I climbed up the rock. The ghost was raging and prophesying and the rest. I'm not surprised Diana was scared stiff. The ghost was there all right. Mad Margaret. So near I could have touched her. And I would have done if some damn fool hadn't knocked me off. The next thing that I knew, I was wet through and trussed up on the bank and the ghost was gone. But a large bird was on the rock, more or less where she'd stood."

"Am I expected to believe this moonshine?"

"Believe what you damned well like. It happens to be true."

"It would be a dreadful thing for sure," said Angus. "I think he must be mad, poor soul, to see the old wife on her rock and turned into a bird. It's true they say the dead fly at the full moon, but that I think I would have noticed. And if I had shot at this callant, I'm thinking I'd have seen the wifey too."

"You call me a liar. You must have seen her; yes, and heard her voice. She talked for ages, pretty loud."

"It's possible," Alastair said thoughtfully, "that his fall may have deranged him."

"I'm as sane as you are," Peter countered furiously, "Though in this mad house that's no recommendation. Everyone knows Glenshael is haunted. If you would condescend to let me go, I assure you I won't set foot in it again. I wouldn't come near this place if you paid me."

"Happen you'll do the paying," offered Angus.

"I doubt it. You haven't got a thing on me. Whereas, from first to last, I've had the works. First that damned ghost upset my girl by slandering me wholesale. Then I was shot at, tied up, and now this treatment. I've done nothing—nothing—and you can't prove otherwise."

"At best you were trespassing, perhaps loitering with intent. We really can't release you. These others think you are a criminal, and I am more and more doubtful of your sanity. No man in his right senses would invent such unlikely excuses, and you seem besides to have a persecution complex. We must obviously shut you up, while we decide what's best to do. Craigie, have we suitable prison handy?"

"The old butler's pantry, sir, would serve the purpose. The windows are barred and there are outside bolts. It's warmer than the cellar."

"Excellent idea," said Alastair.

"But this is iniquitous!" Peter cried. "It's forcible detention. If I'm so dangerous—why not call the police?"

"Our one constable won't thank us if we get him out of bed, and frankly I don't blame him. Really, Smith, you are very ignorant of local custom. We always lock up poachers overnight, it's so much more convenient for

everyone. Also you ought to see a doctor, who needs his
night's rest too. And meanwhile, I suggest that you relax.
It might be unwise to excite yourself. And incidentally,
think up something plausible for the police."

So the fine cat-and-mouse game continued and Peter
was incarcerated for several hours. They made him comfortable, and he took their advice, resigning himself to his
situation and planning for its disentanglement. At dawn
he was despatched down to the village with Angus and
Craigie in attendance. They went on foot towards the
policeman's house but at the main road suddenly grew
careless. Peter was ready and soon shook off pursuit.
Angus took careful aim—and hit a rabbit. They noted
that the fugitive headed towards Stranach, and it was
thought he caught the first southbound train.

Meanwhile I too had had a long night, though we all
seemed to work in cells like red spies. However, the sun
rose on a new day, so I'd better add the story of Deborah.

The first thing I had done was to call David. His crisp
voice made me realize how tired I was. Still, youngsters
don't mind turning night to day. And nor did he.

"You've found her?"

"I know where she is at present. But there's no guaran-
tee she'll stay around. You have a car. Can you come over
here? I'm sure it's urgent, or I wouldn't bother you."

"To Bywater's place?"

"Where else? I'll wait for you outside. I have to talk to
you. I'll tell you then where she is and what has happened." I rang off hastily to leave him in suspense.

It gave me time to tidy up and try out a few stories. I
did not make the same mistake as Peter and cling to the

truth. David at last arrived, and I wasted no more time. I got in the car with him to go on with my story.

"Portneish, you see, is just the place she'd choose. But she might run away again. When I saw her, she was in a thorough panic. She might not wait till morning, as she has a car."

"I don't see why."

"Be your age, David. You've heard about this man by now—the latest fortune hunter. He took her out at night and scared her stiff. The inference is obvious. The way I work it out, you worried him, so he tried another tack."

"Why here?"

"God knows. I'm only telling you he frightened her and she ran off and left him stranded. Are we supposed to wait till he finds his way back and starts the old game from a new angle? When I think of the poor child, with no responsible relations, it upsets me. It really does."

"She has me."

"I realize that, David. That's why I got in touch. You'll know the best line to take, I'm sure. For after all, you understand her."

He didn't mind it laid on thick. He rather liked it. But being David, he worried the bone.

"You know it's after one o'clock? What will they think at the hotel? It's a strange hour for callers. And do we know what name she's using? We might barge in on anyone."

"We'll soon find out," I said optimistically, "and we'll see her if we have to storm the place. David—do you want the girl or not? For if you do, now is the chance to get her. There she is, on the plate, gold-plate at that. You only have to get into her room somehow."

"Hardly, Miss Rayner. It wouldn't be the thing."

"Gracious, how moral! Who the hell cares? You can treat her like a doting brother."

"That's not the point."

"Stop arguing, David, and drive faster. I've had no sleep tonight; I want to get this over, and off-load the burden given me by destiny. Nothing will give me greater pleasure. I'm not an altruist by nature."

We covered some more miles in silence. I nearly went to sleep. I've never felt so chilled and ragged. I groaned at renewed conversation.

"What on earth induced her to get involved with a chap like that?"

"He was a good deal cleverer than she was."

"Not difficult. Though, mind you, Deb has a brain. She got three 'A' levels."

"An inadequate equipment for the school of life."

"She likes clever people. Last time it was a weedy artist who wanted a free berth. Preferred existentialism to water. What's this one's line?"

"Celtic twilight, highland history, and very slick technique. It's understandable. She's insecure and young."

"She's nineteen. In two years' time she'll be of age, and the money isn't tied up properly. Old Mansfield meant the boys to take the lion's share and keep an eye on Deb. God knows what will happen if she doesn't learn some sense. The people she can trust, she doesn't; but she's predisposed towards every crook she meets."

"So you'll have to marry her," I said wearily. "Just use the velvet gloves and stop treating her like a bairn. Anyone would find it irksome. She needs intelligent handling. Look how she purred for Mr. Peter Rannoch. I

should think one might mistake you, David, for a bull-
dozer. If you want to protect her, you must love her
first."

"But I do love her. It's obvious to anyone."

"No need to shout. It ruins the effect. I wouldn't doubt
the quality of your emotion, David, but you have the
oddest way of showing it."

"I don't do badly. I had an operation—right? I rushed
straight from hospital to Anacher. Though I felt grim,
I've been chasing round for days, nonstop. I find Deb tied
up with the usual weed, and all she does is run away from
me. My sick-leave is nearly over, and in a month or two
I'm due to go abroad. If you think I've time for fancy
stuff, you're very much mistaken. I've been very patient
with Deborah, but now she can make up her mind. She
can realize my career's important to me and to my wife,
and money doesn't buy everything."

I eyed the approaching pepperpot turrets of Portneish
with some misgiving. The romance didn't sound too
promising. Yet David was such a suitable young man.
Suitable for what?

"For better or for worse," I murmured thoughtfully.

"Correct. But girls don't like the rough mixed with the
smooth. I'm sorry for Deb in many ways, but she must be
taught to face responsibility."

All very master-race, but the mood seemed to vanish as
soon as we had entered the hotel. It was left to me to take
command, as though I had some natural right to do so.
We were fortunate to find the entrance hall deserted, the
night porter being temporarily away. I made straight for
the register while our luck held, and with dates, initials,

and car number soon had a room marked down for Deborah.

"One-sixty-six. I think that's the first floor. Use the stairs, not the lift, David. Less disturbance. I'll hold the fort here or go back to the car."

"But you must come as well. It's the whole point surely of your being here at all."

"My dear David, she doesn't even know me, she might not trust me, and three's not company, as well you know."

"It doesn't matter. All you have to do is play chaperon. After all, it would look bad if we were on our own."

"To whom? Not me. I try to think the best of everyone."

"You know perfectly well what I mean. I must insist that you come too."

As all this wasted time, I eventually agreed. And I thought I might be required to prod, if things went too askew. We found the room without much trouble but were hampered by David's fondness for propriety. His gentle scratching on the door, his discreet whispering, were probably not heard at all. I took the matter over.

"Who's there?" Deborah's voice was recognizable but muffled. I turned towards David hopefully, but he appeared to have turned to stone.

"Open up, Miss Mansfield, please. It's important. We want to talk to you."

"Go away, whoever you are." And still David said nothing. It made it rather difficult for me.

"I'm a friend of the Macdonalds of Anacher," I tried next. "Also of David Gregory, who's here with me."

"I don't believe you."

"Why not look for yourself?"

"Well, I'm not going to. I'll phone the house detective."

"Deb, stop behaving like a clot and let us in." David had found his tongue at last. "We're practically causing a disturbance. Do you want the whole hotel to know our business?"

It wasn't a way that I'd have chosen to soothe a ruffled girl, but at least it had immediate effect. Strange sounds issued from the other side which ended only when the key was finally turned. The poor child had not relied on locks and bolts but had made a barricade against the door. When it opened, she was framed, swollen-eyed, against a chest of drawers and several chairs. She must have fallen on some boggy ground, for her new holiday clothes were mud-spattered. However, none of this concerned her. She didn't wait until the door was closed behind us but hurtled headlong into David's arms.

"Oh Davy, Davy, darling Davy! I can't believe it's you."

"Of course it's me, you prize idiot! There, there, Twopenny. Don't cry."

This made a few more tears course down her cheeks, while she gasped and sobbed and sniffed.

"Davy, I wanted you so much. You've no idea how badly. I've behaved appallingly. I'm scared. I've got myself into an awful mess. But you will help me, won't you? Please!"

I had meanwhile shut the door and was examining the room. Deborah had not delayed her packing. We had caught her just in time. My guilt was somewhat eased since I had done the right thing. She looked in need of care and protection. I'd have rather been outside than here with them, for their conversation promised to be neither stimulating nor intellectual. But at least the only cursory and suspicious glance my hostess deigned to offer was unaccompanied by fear or recognition.

"Who's she?"

"Miss Rayner found out where you were and got in touch with me."

"I'm a friend of Catherine Macdonald's and she was worried about you. We've been hunting for you since you left Mrs. Morrison's."

"Never mind that." David, for once, helped out. "The thing is, Twopenny, what's been going on?"

"I'm so upset, Davy—utterly miserable—and terribly ashamed. I was horrid to you, Davy, and you're so good to me. I didn't even go to see you in hospital. I shall never forgive myself—never."

"Don't work yourself up, Twopence. Davy understands."

He mopped her eyes with great care but didn't stop the tears.

"You don't at all. I didn't want to visit you. I was afraid you'd make me marry you. I didn't know my own mind then, Davy darling. It seemed tame somehow. But now I don't want any more excitement, ever. I really, really don't."

"Not even on your wedding day, my darling?"

"That's the thing. I can't marry you. I'm engaged to someone else. Only I never want to see him again. What shall I do? If I don't see him, I can't break it off. And I'm scared of him as well. I've got into a muddle, Davy. I don't know how to sort it out."

"I'll sort it out," said David grimly. "You leave it to me, poppet. Who and where is this chap? I'll break it off for you."

"He isn't here. For all I know, *she* drowned him as she said she would. I expect they'll think I did it, for I was with him in the glen, and we've been seen everywhere together since I came up here."

"I can't make head or tail of this. Who is this *she?* And where's this glen?"

"Glenshael, it's called. I'll never set foot in it again. It was horrible, Davy. I was scared right from the first, but he made me go on. Then this ghost came. It's a haunted glen, you see, and she said all sorts of things in a most ghastly voice and told me that I had to marry you."

"Debbie, you're far too old now for such stories."

"It's true. Cross my heart and hope to die. Oh, dear! Perhaps I shouldn't say so!"

"Never mind, darling. We'll discuss it another time, when you feel better. I understand. But we'll forget this chap tonight. You don't have to invent anything."

"If I may say so," I put in before Deborah could enlarge on her apparent fantasies, "that is very good advice. It would be unwise for Deborah to have much more strain. Whatever happened, it seems to have been most unpleasant, and I think, David, she should have a rest. Plenty of time to work it out together. Things will seem better in the morning. However, it does strike me that she shouldn't see this man again at all. He's unlikely to have come to any harm, but he might find his way back here. A rather shoddy youth, I thought; unquestionably bogus, but quite able to look after himself and end up on his feet."

"Thank goodness Davy's here." She snuggled charmingly. "And you won't leave me, will you? Not for a teeny-weeny moment?"

"A tall order, precious, but I can't stay here, you know. However, I'll be over first thing in the morning."

"But you can't *go!* I won't let you." She had been improving, but this lost her ground. Her security depended wholly upon contact. She gripped him like a vise.

He kissed her for about the seventh time. Each essay seemed to last longer. Then, being David, he got down to facts. The lateness of the hour, the bedroom scene. And all she had to do, he said, was lock her door and wait till he came back.

"I won't. I hate this place. I'm coming with you."

"Not possible. I'm staying at Lord Mantum's house, and the only staff in residence are men. It wouldn't do."

"I've been so stupid over Peter, it scarcely matters."

"All the more reason why we must do things properly now. We don't want to start together on the wrong foot. Having got involved with this man Rannoch, what will be said if you then come to live alone with me at Anacher? Or I stay with you in this room? I have your reputation to consider, and you must give some thought to my career."

I did not feel that Deborah was in good shape for such formalities, and the argument as far as I could see might last till morning. Like Deborah, I myself was anxious to be clear of the locality before friend Peter put in an appearance. She might not couple her duenna with a specter, but his head was far clearer.

"Supposing we shut up the suitcases and go *somewhere,*" I suggested. "Deborah has packed to all intents and purposes, and you don't want her to escape again. At worst, we all could drive around till morning, defending reputations right and left. But I do think, David, if we have Deborah in renewed hysterics a disturbance will be caused, and who knows?—people may *talk*."

It was fortunate they had no sense of humour that I understood, and so few sensible ideas that they obeyed me. Back in the car, I dozed at once, and only woke to say *No* firmly to any suggestions which involved me.

I assumed that in the end they'd go to Anacher. She intended that, but he was stubborn. And then illumination came to my weary brain. Anacher! Catherine was getting out of this scot-free. It was time someone took over. I was finished.

"You can drop me at Holly Bank." I thumped David on the back when at last we came to Glenshael. "Your chaperon retires. You're on your own. And don't tell me you're not fit to be in charge of an innocent, for I shan't believe you. You're a phenomenon. A glorious Galahad. And to award such purity of heart, and further your career, I will ring up Ilsafeccan and get a bed for Deborah. She knows Mrs. Macdonald, so she'll be fine."

I sounded sadly like James Bywater.

"We'd better wait to see if it's all right," said David, after some discussion.

"I'd prefer to do so when you were halfway there. It makes refusal more difficult, and you won't know one way or the other. You just arrive and trust to highland hospitality."

I limped into Holly Bank by the back door. My head was splitting and most sensitive. It jangled even at the distant bell, which a sleepy Catherine answered eventually.

"You asked me to look for Deborah. Well, I've found

her and despatched her, complete with boy-next-door, to Ilsafeccan. Don't ask me what to do with her. I don't know. I never want to see the girl again. I don't approve of childhood sweethearts, and I find I have a singularly immoral view on life. He calls her Twopence. Fair warning. If I have to play duenna—a post, I find, for which I'm ill-adapted—give me some lovers I can understand, preferably minus fortunes or careers. What else? I can't think straight. I've had no sleep all night. Ah yes, she rubs her nose on his lapel."

"Where did you pick her up? And what of Peter?"

"I neither know nor care, and nor need you. Just be a kind lady chieftain and air a bed for her. After which, arrange a wedding. It should be child's play."

"Sherlock wins through! How wonderful! Elementary, I suppose."

"I'm sorry, Watson, but you always get the rough end. But one thing, I don't need cocaine tonight."

I've never flopped so thankfully in bed. Not only was I utterly exhausted, but I had that smug pleasure in a task accomplished. I'd been a thought fey about that girl from the beginning. Damned nuisance, but she'd had her uses after all. Strange to have been involved so deeply. Strange to have turned the full circle back to my beginnings. What did it mean? Where did it start and end?

In a railway train? Or in Glenshael? Or nowhere?

# 16

## Fly Not Yet

I was late for breakfast and began my day with an apology. James was not pleased with me.

"I'm surprised you managed to come down at all," he grumbled. "Are you sufficiently rested? It is not usual in the country to arrive home after four."

"So late?" I parried.

"Not that it is necessary to adopt their loathsome habits. Still, one does try to compromise. Besides, I had a shocking night. My neuralgia resolved itself to toothache. When at last I did drop off to sleep, you woke me up."

"Oh, James, I'm sorry. Feel better this morning?"

"Worse," he replied in deepest gloom, and took two codeine tablets.

"Yes, I see your jaw looks very swollen." It was, in fact, a trifle difficult to judge the curves of James's moon-face. "Is it a back tooth?"

"Tooth! I have two of them, both raging. One I've had trouble with before. I expect I shall now lose both."

"Have you made an appointment with the man in Stranach?"

"That butcher! No thank you, my dear Alice. I am not a hero of the dentist's chair. However, I must be attended to. I shall set out for Fort John. I do hope I haven't an abscess. I don't feel a bit well, you know."

"I'll drive you if you like."

"I detest being driven, as you know, especially by women who are short of sleep. No, I shall take the train and tolerate your taxi service to the station. It will be less draughty, and I may get some sleep if I drug myself sufficiently. I'm afraid an extraction is inevitable. Perhaps I ought to stay the night."

So in fact, I was so busy wrapping him up in scarves, reserving him a room and an appointment, the morning passed quickly, with only a most superficial account of the night's events. You couldn't blame the man for taking no great active interest in Deborah's affairs. Love seems unlikely when you have the toothache.

I decided to have lunch at Mrs. Morrison's, for by then I felt real need for nourishment and strong black coffee. There was no rush now to get home, and once my sleepiness wore off I felt better a few miles from Glenshael. I took my tangled thoughts out walking by the loch. Now Deborah was settled, I had no excuse to stay. Back to bed-sitting rooms again, to rush-hour tube trains, and oblivion.

"Good afternoon, Miss Rayner," said a voice beside me.

"Mr. Macdonald!" I jumped guiltily.

"In search of exercise? Well, so am I. We can walk, perhaps, together."

"Such a delightful afternoon. But I was intending to sit by the loch. I'm no great walker."

"Then I'll sit with you. I have several bones to pick."

"I'm not surprised. I'm sorry about last night. But I had reached the end of my tether. I do hope your wife will one day forgive me, but she was concerned about young Deborah, and I know so few people in this district. They did arrive, I gather?"

"They did indeed. Entwined like luscious woodbine. As pretty a scene as I have ever seen. There is a very minor question. Will you accompany them on their honeymoon —or is that an extension of our duty? If so, we'd better get conditioned. At present, it is more than enough for me to witness their impassioned clinches. More I dare not envisage, but I hope to grow far less particular with practice."

"But everything goes smoothly?"

"I doubt if she will change lovers for a week or two," he said. "I'd find it disconcerting myself, but some folk are adaptable. At any rate, the Rannoch fellow's out, coupled now in her mind for good and all with the Specter of the Glen."

"Heavens! Does she still persist with that tale in broad daylight? I imagined it hysteria."

"That's what young David thinks, but Catherine and I have now heard the story several times; the detail always tallies. And there are a lot of interesting points. Moreover, she believes it. It's very touching really. There she was going up the glen towards her doom, and coming down an altered person. At last she knew who it was she really loved, for richer or for poorer. Catherine goggles. That sort of thing's right up her street."

"Ghosts?"

"Not exactly. Pseudo-specters, who intervene to save on fate's instructions."

"Too complicated for my simple mind. I believe merely in imagination. Peter had told her about Mad Margaret until she thought she saw her."

"But she didn't. She saw Aillie Rannoch. These southrons are so ignorant. Who else would she see in Glenshael, and at the full moon too?"

"One ghost is just like another, as far as I'm concerned. Deborah may feel that as well."

"Yet it's an interesting study, Miss Rayner. Even ghosts differ, sometimes markedly. Of course, I knew Aillie well. She made an excellent spae-wife. I mind one day—up by the broch at Anachsaig. She scared a fat American, wee devil. I really thought he'd have a heart attack."

"Alive or dead, she always sounds eccentric."

"Volatile just. What else could she have been with that upbringing? Spoilt to distraction one day, skelped the next; reared like a boy and treated like a man, and she a wee and rather lonely girl forbye. My mother always said it was a miracle she turned out so well, but she had great courage and resolution, Aillie."

I was silent, partly because I cast about for some way out of this, mostly because my tiredness made tears seem so easy.

"Nevertheless, she did the silliest things, there was no stopping her. I thought once she'd kill herself from sheer bravado. You'd think she would grow out of it, but no. She still crops up in grave clothes to scare foreigners. But did you scare the Rannoch claimant? That's the point. To speak frankly, puss, I'm glad to see you alive."

"Have you been stringing me along, Anacher?"

"I'd like fine to answer *yes*, but so help me! I swallowed Miss Alice Rayner whole. What sort of fool does that make me, I'm wondering? I only clicked last night when Deborah was talking. Then it all fell in place, for it's not as if you look so different basically. Seeing you just now in the town, there was no doubt at all. Mind, you're a damned good actress, you always were, and what you don't expect, you don't look out *for*."

"Contrariwise," I said. "It worked with Deborah. Nearly with Peter, but not quite. However, Angus took him over, and I had a message that he up and ran."

"Good riddance! But this other game, Aillie. What the hell are you playing at?"

"But nothing, Robin. I was homesick. I saw James Bywater's advertisement, and that was that. It all worked in so well. What James needed served as my disguise. I didn't want to set up as a Rannoch. I just wanted to see Glenshael again. It's all right for you, Robin, you come and go. I hadn't had a glimpse for ten long years. And yet I didn't want to cause a stir at all."

"What optimism! As if you could help it. You always did plunge order into chaos. It's a sort of gift you have— not from the gods."

"I have done nothing."

"Aillie, Aillie! Ask your Fause Rannoch what he says to that. I suppose McDhui's in the secret. Anyone else?"

"No, only you, dear cousin Anacher. And don't you dare say anything to anyone."

"You forget, puss, that I'm married, and quite frankly

I don't hold with lack of candour. I haven't yet told
Catherine, but I shall. It's absolutely necessary."

"But no one else? Please, Robin!"

"If no one had known, I'd give you a better chance,
Aillie; but once secrets crack, they run like ice fissures.
Remember that I guessed without help from you. And I
doubt if you are quite as much the schoolmarm as you
were. It's one thing to masquerade a day or two, but not
for long where you are so well kent. The story of the
ghost will get about. Others might have the same reaction."

"No matter. I am leaving anyhow. For the very reasons
which you give. Angus is safe. If you and Catherine play
it my way, I'll get clear, never fear."

"So you run away? That's not like you, Aillie. I'd have
never thought you'd shelve responsibility. You must have
seen things aren't right in Glenshael. It's haunted right
enough—and by your family. The fact is, all these ghosts
are damned unhealthy."

"What can be done?" I shrugged. "These things happen."

"They are your people, Aillie. Good folk too. You
forget it was a bad time for them as well. They have you
on their minds perpetually like a lead weight. Have you
forgotten the curse laid upon them?"

"A hurt child's blether!"

"Aye, but effective. You have lain upon the conscience
ever since. Can you not see now how they felt? They
knew fine you were too young to bear such tragedy, and
they took the blame to lighten it. It was the only way you
could be helped. No one could touch you; you were a
snarl of pain. So they took on all the long mismanage-

ment, the scandal, and the stupid thoughtlessness. They
let you curse them, so you could be eased and find a way
to go. If our sort of background and traditions mean
anything—and I believe they do—the time has come for
you to make a cancellation, not slink away and let them
rot, your friends and neighbours, Aillie."

"Don't nag me, Robin. Do you think that I don't
understand? But it's easier said than done. My own
problems made a mess of it. I had to sort them first. This
made me start all wrong, postpone the broader love till
last. The time's not come. I know my own. They must
never realize I fooled them. An interesting legend, yes,
but one I'd not have told. I should have come back
openly, perhaps, but I wasn't ready for it."

"You always did act back to front."

"I can't help it. It's only since I came back I've understood myself. You stopped me from following Father,
Robin. But I died just the same. Glenshael, it seems, has
resurrected me. No harm in that eventually. But I think
I'll come to terms with Aillie Rannoch first, and meanwhile I'm better out the way."

"You talk in riddles."

"Aye, Robin, let them lie unsolved."

"I wonder. It is on my mind you came here for some
purpose. Did a Macdonald ever trust a Rannoch? And
your behaviour's odd. What were you doing in the glen so
late? All grave clothes and with Angus too? Even Deborah, I noticed, didn't know that Peter planned the expedition. Could it be your object to give Glenshael an even
worse name than it has? And remove all usurpers by the
method? Angus, is it? An ill-friend to Alastair, as well I

know. And to think we introduced you to your vengeance!"

"What are you saying, Anacher?"

"That Forres is a better local influence than your
father. You Rannochs had your chance and lost it. I am
not blaming you. You reaped another's bad harvest. But
Aillie, it is far too late to mend."

"Would I think of such a thing?"

"Yes," he said candidly. "You would. I doubt if you've
improved at all, Aillie Rannoch. Just look how you dealt
with Deborah's Peter, and I bet you enjoyed it too. Don't
tell me that you care a damn about the girl and her
happy future. You were out to oust the man for your own
satisfaction. What else have you been up to?"

"Nothing, Robin. That's the whole point. Peter kept
my fingers out the real pie. The rest I thought I might
digest at my leisure. In London, preferably."

"So you really are going?"

"I am planning my withdrawal."

"Aillie, you're not to disappear again. Let me know
where you go."

"I may or I may not. I'll think about it. However,
perhaps you'll have a Christmas card. To the Napoleon of
the Glens, I think, from his very loving cousin, Aillie
Rannoch."

I drove back thoughtfully. Nothing improved. Ice fissures! The idea stayed with me. Robin had *clicked;*
Catherine would be enlightened; and Angus—what of
him? The thaw was in the air. I knew it. I felt like
absconding with the car and pushing south to safety.

In fact, I headed towards Angus's cottage, anxiety
outweighing discretion. But he was far too intent on his

own contribution to the previous night's work, and without betraying questions I could not decide the real attitude of Alastair. Still, the story amused me, and I was glad of company. I put off going back to Holly Bank.

When I sat down alone at last, my lack of sleep caught up on me. I didn't go at once to bed. Too many stairs. Here I could listen to the waves sough gently in the silence. They reminded me of Debussy and Miss Lamont. I closed my eyes to hear her better. She had a gentle touch. The Feraghan was on the floor again, the wee dogs in the cabinet, and my little beadwork stool beside the fire was occupied, and I asking questions, everlastingly, the way I always did.

"Why do you live here, Miss Lamont?"

But she just smiled.

"Is it because of Father?" Funny, I'd never thought of that before, yet now I saw quite plainly how it was.

She didn't answer, but she changed the tune. A new one, very dreich.

"Don't be sad, Miss Lamont. I canna bear it. Why can't folk be happy? Why can't you?"

"I am happy, Aillie. There's an art in learning how. Besides, it happened a long time ago, before you, child, were born. Everyone thought—but then your mother came along. She was a vivid creature. No man could resist her."

"Ach, well she didn't last so very long, I'm thinking. You could still marry Father, Miss Lamont."

"What's marriage, child? You will learn, in your turn, you can't dictate to love. Or will you? Dougal never did. You are a strange breed. Yes, Aillie. I could have been his second choice more or less any time these last ten years. I

couldn't do it, Aillie. I couldn't forgive; either past dis-
appointments or present weaknesses. So I compromised. I
failed him but never you, the Rannoch child that I myself
had wanted. I swore that you should always have a
second home and the security of sense. I haven't let you
down, have I? I meant it for the best."

"Miss Lamont!" She faded and I was alone, rubbing
my eyes, the dream still with me. I had come back to my
second home for sure—to Holly Bank. Yes, here I was. A
vivid dream. Somehow it could be true. The more I
thought, the more convinced I was. Life's strange. Miss
Lamont and Father! She'd loved him faithfully but without respect. A generous woman, mourning for a rake,
rearing a rival's bairn with selfless love.

I hoped she knew that I appreciated this great honour,
that I wished I was more like her, more the way she'd
planned. Ach, but I had to be myself—as she had been. It
worried me to think of her long disappointment. The
Rannochs of Glenshael weren't much to love.

Just the same, I could feel her safety wrapping round
me. I curled up smiling and remembered her. The quiet
smile, the aching or the vulnerable.

She was a fine woman, Miss Lamont.


James Bywater came back next day. I went to meet
him at the station and together we relived each moment
of his agony which lost him two fine molars. He was
gratified when I suggested he should go to bed and nurse
himself with care. My salary I earned by cooking invalid
food and dosing him with pills.

"You're a treasure, my dear Alice."

"Yes, James, I always thought so, but it's nice to know my night rambling's forgiven."

He grinned. Although a little pale, he was far more his old self.

"And I quite like you organizing me. I resign myself to bossy women. They seem to be my lot."

"You like being fussed over. And now I think that you should go to sleep."

"Bunkum! I'm perfectly restored, now I am off my legs. No work today, perhaps, but conversation."

"Very well, here's a topic. I heard in Stranach yesterday that Margie Cameron, the Episcopalian minister's first-born, is looking for a job. She has been convalescing from some illness and wants to stay around, but she did work for a London publisher. Imagine that."

"Why should it interest me?"

"I've been thinking, James. You could do worse. There just isn't the work here for an efficient resident. Now Margie could go home when you were meditating, instead of meddling round the house. No problem about leisure. Less money. And all that hard experience."

"I might not deserve such a prodigy."

"You don't deserve me, James, I'll tell you that. I'm hopeless for any length of time. I'm sure I'm ruining your chapters. You can feel me writing them my own way. You said yourself that I was interfering. And really, James, I am."

"In other words, you want to leave?"

"Yes, James; I do. And Margie would be better. She's very sensible and crisp. I was at school with her in the old days. She's very clever. She used to come to our dominie to learn Greek."

"Your dominie? Just where was that?"

"I'd better tell you. I feel bad about this. James, I've done some stupid things in my time, but now I've over-reached myself. I went to school here in Glenshael. Alison Rannoch is my real name. I'm not a typist; I'm a ghost. I don't suppose you've ever met one socially."

"The girl Aillie? Well, well, well!"

"I'm not your type at all, James. I'm too melodramatic. I curse folk in the Gaelic and I walk in moonlit glens. I believe I would affect your style, James, after a while. You wouldn't like that, would you?"

"No one recognized you?"

"Not at first, so I believed that it could work. I told you I had been an actress. There's a lot in technique. But I was too ambitious. First Angus McDhui, and now my Cousin Anacher, who in turn will tell his wife. Too many, James, in a close neighbourhood like this. I'd better run before I am a nine days' wonder. I'm sure that you don't wish to house a freak show."

"Frankly, no, and certainly not you."

"May I telephone Miss Cameron then?"

"Not so fast, my dear Alice. You have put me where you want me. But have you anywhere to go?"

"Nowhere since I was sixteen, James. But I've always managed, and I will again. I can do nearly anything, you know. I've scrubbed and typed and cooked and been a waitress. Bread is a great incentive. I can act. I am very good at selling things in shops. I'm wasted on you, James."

"You must be only twenty-six."

"And Margie's twenty-five. You'll like her, honestly.

She has advanced views, they say—reaction to the
Manse. I'm so old-fashioned, James. I'm getting worse."

"Poor Alice. What a meek and modest role! You win,
the avant-garde Greek scholar is accepted. You're right in
this, my dear. You *are* disturbing. You have made me
need another aspirin. Or two would be better."

I telephoned the eldest Miss Cameron, I retyped the
ruined chapter, I tidied the workroom, and I packed my
clothes. I was conscious all the time that things were too
smooth altogether; I was conscious that I ought to go to
Castle Rannoch, but my shoulders wouldn't square. The
sword of Damocles seemed poised above my head, and
when the doorbell rang I thought it fell.

It was only Catherine Macdonald.

"I'll take back everything I ever said about Alastair."
She spoke rather rapidly, as if to ward off awkwardness.
"I called in at the castle to borrow a report Robin
wanted. He nearly bit my head off. You don't look much
more welcoming, after all I've done for you."

"How are the turtledoves?"

"Cooing away. The wedding bells are pealing in our
ears. St. Margaret's and white marquisette. We're doing
excellently. I feel like a missionary who has saved a soul
from sin, but you don't look so jubilant yourself."

"I'm grateful to hear you take them in your stride. It
was a dreadful imposition. You might well have been
furious."

"Robin was—absolutely livid—until Deb started on
her ghost story. I thought he was deranged, the way he
laughed, but he only said there was one born every
minute. I thought he meant his guest—or wife—until last
night."

"A prize bitch, Catherine. How right you were. But it's fine to know that Robin has good taste."

"I still can't believe it. It's incredible!"

"I shall vanish as I came, and soon you will have dreamt it."

"Aillie, we think that you should come to Ilsafeccan. Deborah will soon be going. Robin too. He's due one of his round trips. It would look natural to invite a friend to keep me company. And I would rather like to know you better."

"One day we'll get acquainted, Catherine. Thank you, just the same."

"You sound as valedictory as Alastair. I don't think he cares to hear about my lovebirds. I don't think that he cares for me. Perhaps he found my presence *compromising*. Or do you think David is affecting me?"

"You didn't mention my part in the matter, I hope."

"I daren't. What with Robin swearing me to secrecy and Mr. Forres all scowls. I wouldn't like to have high jinks in his glen. Trespassing, Aillie. Shocking!"

After she'd gone, I cooked some more for James, who appeared absorbed in Dostoyevsky. There wasn't very much to do, except to call myself a coward.

It nagged me that Alastair had been so brusque with Catherine. Something was irking him back to old ill-humour. I hoped he wouldn't take it out on Angus. The old man wouldn't think to tell on me. If anything happened, I would be to blame. Alastair, guessing he'd been tricked, might lose his patience. Sourpuss! How long ago it seemed. *Flowers of the Amazon*. A sort of magpie.

Very well, I'd go. I'd conduct myself with great decorum—and incidentally see him one more time. He wouldn't smile perhaps, but never mind. I could say goodbye—a word which meant nothing. I could play the last act of my masquerade and watch the curtain fall. Exit Miss Rayner. Exit everyone.

And no new play in sight.

# 17

## Woo'd,

## Married, and a'

ALASTAIR, WEARING HORN-RIMMED spectacles, sat at his desk in the book room. He might have been a headmaster and I some small offender needing punishment, an effect which was enhanced as he did not rise but finished off a sentence with a flourish of his pen. It came to me I'd never seen his handwriting. I wouldn't know it on an envelope. Ten days is an ungenerous allotment. No wonder there were gaps.

"So you've come at last?"

"I was passing. I dropped in to see you."

"How very gratifying. Why not yesterday?"

"Because I was in Stranach."

I shifted from one foot to the other and glared at him. Treat me like a schoolgirl, I'd behave like one!

"You could have telephoned." He stood up now, only to look down on me disdainfully.

"Why should I, Alastair? I had no reason . . ."

"Except common courtesy," he interrupted. "Don't you think some apology was due? You prize me out of bed to play idiotic games with your ridiculous associates. I stay up all night, illegally detaining your *bête noir*. Yet you have neither the politeness to give some briefing nor the good manners to let me know the outcome. I have to wait till Catherine Macdonald gives me details—or did you delegate the job to her? I suppose you think I should be flattered at being offered a small walk-on part entirely without cues. Believe me, I am not."

"I'm sorry, Alastair, but how was I to know you would connect me with the night's work at all?"

"How stupid do you think I am? Who else could have brought it off in just that way? Did you enjoy your comeback, Anna Rayner? Glenshael is honoured you should choose it for your benefit performance. Though what a pity to waste your talent on such shabby audience, entirely free of charge."

"You're a bastard right enough, Alastair. I did it for charity. The lack of charity I left to you. An excellent choice."

"I understand you frightened Deborah out her wits. A kind act, I'm sure. And the wonder is the young man wasn't killed outright. The whole thing was so questionable, I daren't inform the police. God knows what you were doing in the glen so late—but to tackle them in such a fashion! Anything might have happened. You were damned lucky, don't you realize?"

"A lot of fuss about nothing."

"Nothing! I gather that he nearly had you, and we don't know his range. If he's not a criminal, he's pretty near it, and playing for big money. Supposing he had recognized you? Not had that small doubt? You were inviting murder. Can't you see?"

"I can't see what concern it is of yours."

"It's my glen and I like to keep it corpse-free. And it wouldn't occur to you perhaps that I was worried stiff all night. I gathered that you needn't be extinct, though I was glad to hear next morning you were whole. I understand that, frightened, you'd not run to me for comfort. I merely say you might have got in touch."

"At the time I had to follow up the girl, which took most of the night. Next morning James was ill and I busy. If I'd realized you'd put two and two together I would have rung you up, though I couldn't have said much on the telephone."

"Did that man touch you?"

"No, the ubiquitous McDhui dealt with him while I got away. What happened to the villain of the piece? Does anybody know?"

"He'll be sitting pretty, far away, hatching out blackmail schemes."

"Oh, no!" Though it seemed very likely.

"However, I've been in touch with Deborah's lawyers and dropped a hint to an old friend who works in Scotland Yard. Mr. Smith-Rannoch would be unwise to start up anything afresh and would be well advised to graze new pastures. Beyond that I don't meddle. My sympathy, such as it is, lies with the victim. He has done nothing wrong, after all, so far, but tell fairy tales—a hobby in which he is outclassed by others I know better. As for you, I warn you. In future, if you need my help, please ask for it. It appears that you acquired delusions of grandeur in more halcyon days, and lose your glamour hard."

"Not even fair! Who may I have glamoured, for God's sake?"

"McDhui, for one. A most unlikely person. You two were hand in glove, yet by all logic he should be furious that you impersonated what he holds in reverence. He's half-mad about his holy relics. Another thing which rather worries me."

"Natural. He heard Peter claim to be Glenshael. He'd forgive anyone who helped to bring him low."

"Don't be too sure. Temporarily, perhaps. But now will he absolve you or plan revenge?"

"A purely academic question, for I'm off back to London. That's really why I came—to say goodbye. I think I've found a substitute for James. So there's nothing to keep me here."

"No?"

"No, Alastair. You're free of my high hand from now on. A pity. I did hope to part more cordially than we met, remembering your kindness in between."

"If that's an exit line, I'm not impressed. Why don't you look me in the face when you speak to me?"

I did so promptly and defiantly.

"It's good enough for you," I said. He could still make me wild, Alastair. "I've been most civil all along, but you haven't said one decent word to me. You go on and on. You treat me like a bairn. And I'll tell you this, I will be glad to see the last of you."

"The last of me? You're going to London. I spend a lot of time there. I have a flat in Regent's Park."

"What's that to do with it?"

"Does your reputation worry you in London? We'd be freer there."

I stared at him. I'd always thought of Alastair at Castle Rannoch, and Glenshael separate from the wider world. The possibility of interchanging them had not occurred to me. A lingering child's-eye view.

"I shall not leave a forwarding address," I said haughtily. "When I don't want to see folk, they don't see me. I'm not inexperienced, as you have gathered. And London is the finest hiding place of all."

"Why should you wish to hide from me? I thought we were friends."

"Friends!" I exploded. "We don't behave like them."

"Lovers then?" He was laughing at my tone of voice and spoke very softly.

"We are not! Alastair, keep away from me! We're enemies."

He put his arms around me and his cheek on mine. "I always treat my enemies like this. Oh, darling, I am sorry. I've behaved abominably, but I've finished being bad-tempered—really! I can't help it. I worry so about you—about us. If only you could trust me, and tell the truth occasionally, I'd feel better. There's so much trouble in your face. Couldn't you look a bit more bridal, my wee love, before I offer you my hand and heart?"

"You mustn't do that, Alastair. I'd only refuse. I would!"

"Could you tell me why? You owe that to me. You realize, as I do—this is special. We could be so very happy. You love me, don't you?"

I made no reply. I shook free wearily and went over to the window. Tears blurred my vision without falling, strangely impressionistic. For instance, Angus crossed the lawn, a big fish in his hand. He might have been much younger with his loping stride, the roses might have been unpruned, the smooth turf rough again. It used to be a paradise for children, secret and overgrown.

"What a trim suburban plot," I said irrelevantly.

"As mistress of Castle Rannoch you could change it."

"Wrong tense; wrong mood. I used to be. In a way I still am. I can call up spirits in the glen and issue orders to retainers. Not power I want—power I cannot lose. A chained, tutelary guardian. My father too. He shot himself where you trail *Clematis montana*. I'm glad, mind, you cut down that shrubbery. It always had a queer dead smell. He's buried now. It took ten years to reconsecrate the ground."

"I should have guessed," I heard him say.

"Not necessarily. You were diverted, Alastair, most usefully so. At first I got away with it completely, but now the rot is setting in. You're the fifth person in the secret. That's why I daren't stay longer. No point in everybody knowing. I only made this daft return to come to grips with old unhappiness."

"Yes, I do understand. Please accept my profound apologies. I've been vain and presumptuous. Amusing! I'm not usually obtuse, but ignorance is confusing. I can see now you could hate me on principle, and I could mistake the emotion's nature. Enemies indeed. But console yourself. I find your revenge most adequate. Fifth on your list. An also-ran. Hoist with my wishful thinking."

I swung round now. "It was not deliberate. It happened—it just happened. Angus was bound to spot me, Robin recognized my spae-wife act, and he told Catherine, as was natural. It snowballs, that's the trouble. I can't stop it. That's why I have to get away."

"But not meet me in London? One, two, three. Would I be allowed to know the fourth?"

"I'm letting James down badly. He'd a right to know why."

"You told Bywater? Good God! No doubt quite voluntarily, when I had to wring it out of you. One step ahead of me. Lucky man! How did he take it? Perfectly, as usual, dear, dear James? Or was he embarrassed to find Glenshael his private dog's body?"

"You're jealous! Ach, how absurd!"

"I'm surprised that he takes precedence. You play your cards all wrong, Miss Rannoch. You could have reeled me in, together with your home, your old position, your glen, your precious Shael, and even your damned salmon. I'm a good match. I've far more money than Rannochs ever had. Worth making a very satisfactory cast. What made you lose your nerve?"

"How dare you talk like that to me? How dare you? You've a tongue like an adder, I am thinking. I don't deserve this, Alastair. I've never meant you any harm. It's not my fault you came into my life when I was too muddled to think straight. But this is true, I wouldn't dream of *landing* you—I never have. They'd all say I'd come home to do just that. I can't help being Aillie Rannoch, but I can help marrying you. And I will."

"Don't you mean *won't?*" He handed me his handkerchief with cool civility. "Perhaps you're wise. I'm far too old for you and more of a crock than I admit."

"Ach, don't be a damned fool, Alastair. Of all the idiotic things to say! Bad enough being sorry for myself;

don't you start too. I wouldn't care if you were bedridden or a hundred plus. If you lived in a hovel or hadn't got a penny. Must we have other complications? It's hell enough already."

"So you do love me?" he asked slowly.

"Of course I do! First time I saw you in that railway train—but that doesn't make me marry you. I don't know why you bother. You're well quit of the Rannochs. You know yourself we're damned bad stock, and I run true to type."

I'd begun to feel a nightmare unreality. Unresolved hurt and tension anchored us. The very air between us was inhibitive, as I circled to avoid the main issue. Yet it was there, dark and menacing. I began to see that there was no escape.

"To hell with the Rannochs! They don't mean a thing to me—nor, I suspect, to you either. I want the truth, Aillie. Let's get it over. Remember that it's you I love—just *you*."

"And who am I? You only know Miss Rayner. My sort of love's not pretty. I'm jealous; I am utterly possessive. By temperament or temper, I'm no wife for anyone. You said I'd henpeck—a fine hen for sure! It's a bird of prey I'd be, with cruel talons. I would want all of you; I'd try and take it. I'd be driven nearly daft with half measures."

"What are you trying to say? Half measures? Look, Aillie, the more possessive that you are with me, the better I'll be pleased. Stop crying, love, and finish with this nonsense. Half measures, hell!"

"Yes, hell for you. I wouldn't do it to you. You talk of love, and so do I, but we mean something different. I need the stars or nothing. I'll not rest with less. I'm trying to

be honest for us both. I would not make a useful housekeeper or bedfellow. You need a decent, generous woman
for that job. You haven't any stars left to give me, and I
like playing lead. I'm sorry. It shames me I can talk like
this; I never meant to. But you asked for it—you drove
me to it—here it is. She'd always be between us; you
belong to her; she's still your wife, I know."

It was dark now. This gave me excuse to draw the
curtains, for some sort of action was imperative. A single
reading lamp shed a quite unjustifiably rosy light. The
fire danced with mocking domesticity. I've never felt so
dreadful, but I braced my shoulders wearily. I must finish
off what I had done—finish.

"Truth at the bottom of the well," I added far more
steadily. "Are you surprised it's murky? It often is. Why
don't you make a renewed declaration of your love, Alastair? Why not *you* speak the truth, play honest, for a
change?"

He struck me straight across the cheek. It hurt like hell
and was the last thing I expected. I was given no time,
though, to show fury or surprise. He followed through in
words.

"You grudging little bitch! You might well be shamed!
Yes, I'll play honest, if you wish. I'll tell you something. I
loved you—God knows why! You meant more to me than
anyone before. Why, heaven knows; I don't. You've lied
and tricked and cheated all along. I think I guessed it,
but I didn't care. You stirred some depth of me I didn't
even know that I possessed. I was prepared to hurt myself
to save your little finger. Payment, however heavy,
seemed quite natural. It was like waking to a new life, but
there was an old one. Fool that I was, I wanted truth

between us. It seemed a generous honest love and worth a little candour. I told you the story of a raw boy's first maturing—of a girl as naïve as the other Deborah. It wasn't complex, or exacting, our short marriage. I said that we were happy—and we were. Poor mite! She had so little and deserved so much. Would you have me deny her what she owned? Whoever I was then, she kept. He died as well; youth does. I am what I am now, what I've become. Thank God we don't all stick at sixteen! My past is my concern and will remain so. I offered you the present and the future. With this proviso, Aillie Rannoch: I'd rather lose you than my self-respect."

I'd rather not describe his voice. His face was empty. This was the real Rannoch curse—to destroy what you loved out of mere lack of self-restraint. The stars had been there all the time, and I had cancelled them. Of all the fools! Of all the bloody fools!

I nearly whimpered. My knees sagged queerly. I wondered if they would collapse and I'd find myself like French tragedy, bathing his feet with tears. This appalling prospect stiffened my spine slightly and fanned a little anger, against myself at least.

"Fine talk!" I managed to retaliate. "Depths, is it? Pretty murky ones! Let this be a lesson to you, Mr. Forres. A man of your age to be glamoured by an ignoble savage. But like Deborah Mansfield it's infatuation, I am thinking. You'll soon be over it, your silly lapse forgotten. No need to back out so ungracefully; I won't embarrass you. You sounded too elegiac, Mr. Forres. I don't like love lukewarm."

I thought my other cheek would have the same treatment. He blazed like murder. Perhaps he didn't trust

himself. The anger flared, catching me up like phos-
phorus, to make a flame of passion. There was no keeping
us apart in love or hate. At last there was contact. I
fought him, yes—glad I must lose. I never knew he had
such strength. I'd met my master at long last. Me, Aillie
Rannoch! A thought untamed and violent—well, why
not? Civilization's too exacting. I loved him too well. And
he loved me. I knew it now. The danger was all gone—the
fire warm and consuming. It was the alloy we had longed
to form—the finer, stronger product.

"Aillie, my dearest love—you belong to me—you do."

"I know, Alastair. I know!"

"We've come through, darling. Can you credit it? I was
so afraid at one stage. We must never be like that again."

"It was only that I loved you so abominably, and it
hurt so much to lose you. And I couldn't bear to make
you miserable."

"You had a darn good try!"

"I want you to be happy, Alastair."

"My dear love, was I happy till you came? And what
on earth would life by like without you? I don't know
what you've done to me, but you're all I want and need,
now and always."

"We're sure to quarrel, Mr. Forres."

"Then we'll make it up like this, and almost worth it. I
don't suppose now we are straighter it will happen often,
but if it does it's part of us. Ach, Aillie love, we won't
escape each other. You're mine, and I'm all yours from
this time on. As for the stars, they're in your eyes already,
and very beautiful they are."

It sounded rather muffled, for he'd bowed his head

against me and I slowly stroked his funny magpie hair. My bonnie Alastair! I never had another doubt again.

Time drifted by and is best not described. We didn't note its passing. It was Craigie who called us from cloud-cuckoo-land by announcing dinner in near desperation.

"I've laid a place, sir, for Miss Rayner."

We'd forgotten she existed.

"The name, it seems, is Rannoch, Craigie; though not, I think, for long."

I could be glad to see the imperturbable surprised, though I could hardly blame him. It is unusual to have ghosts at table. Aunt Ishbel always laid for Uncle Archie, but she was daft, as I told Alastair.

"Well, so are we," he said. "Craigie—champagne, I think."

And once again we were relaxed, gay, though we smiled more than we laughed in our new ease.

"Your health, my love, and mine," he said later. "I'm looking forward very much to you and me."

"To my new part." I smiled. "The douce wife."

"Wife," he corrected. "Don't be too ambitious."

When dinner was over, we strolled down to the glen and listened to the Shael, that most efficient matchmaker. Alastair's moon was still above the trees; my stars were everywhere—no end to them.

We talked a lot of nonsense. We still do. We like it. It's our language.

Not that we needed many words. Love's bonnie when it's new.

But in the end a lucid moment came of reasonable sanity.

"What's the time, Alastair? Is it dreadfully late? I must go home."

"You *are* home, love, in every way."

"Sounds wonderful, but it's a fallacy. I can't stay here all night."

"Much as you'd like to?"

"Ach, Alastair! I said no such thing. It would be most improper."

"I should have thought it more proper to be here with me than under the same roof as James Bywater. Relative, love—an interesting point. I wonder if the village would approve of Aillie Rannoch, compromised by the London 'author body,' especially when she's betrothed to me. You think it over. It's too off-beat for me."

"Alastair! You're absolutely right. This is far worse than David on convention. Well, now perhaps you see that I was not exaggerating. It's a sad coil; even worse now I have dragged you in."

"Let's hope it teaches you to look before you leap," he said unsympathetically. "That is, of course, with everyone but me."

"It's not funny, Alastair. It's complicated. My getaway becomes even more urgent. But I must tie up the loose ends—which means Holly Bank. For I'm not going to run to Ilsafeccan for a chaperon. And yet I'm scared, Alastair. Every step is tricky. I wish I'd gone already."

"Ghosts dematerialize," he murmured lazily.

"Aye, but they're made of ectoplasm. I am not. I wish with all my heart that solid flesh could melt. Or something disentangling happen anyhow. Alastair, would it not be fine if these were the old days? So I could leave a note on my pincushion, and knot my sheets and kilt my petticoats, and fly with my true love beneath a waning moon."

"One needs adaptability, I see, to court a Rannoch."

"When I was a wee girl, I thought it quite the right way to behave. I fancied being thrown across a saddlebow onto a great black horse which galloped through the night."

"Darling, I have neither horse nor saddlebows. But why worry with detail? A Jaguar is even more poetic— symbolic riding of the tiger, as it were. And no dismounting, Aillie love. I see I must abduct you."

He was laughing at me, ruffling my hair, and yet I sensed decision.

"Do you mean elope? Really? With you?"

"Who else? You asked for it."

"But, Alastair—it's wildly idiotic."

"Why then, love, so are we. Particularly you. Go on— say you'll do it! It answers everything with great simplicity."

"But when?"

"Tonight, of course. Beneath the waning moon. Surely real Rannochs don't procrastinate. What have your 'old days' got that we can't better? I'm glad I'm living now."

"Alastair, please be serious."

"I've never been more serious. I doubt if I should let you out my sight. It's not only the Glenshael tangle, though I know it worries you, but you've had an overdose of strong emotion for days now, and I have only piled on more complications. I don't want you reacting all alone, love. I must be near you, Aillie, very near you, so we'll start in harness. The idea is to readjust together at our own speed, and have a rest from outside complications."

"You're being kind again, Alastair."

"To myself, at least. I couldn't bear to lose you now I've found you. So let's get compromised and married thoroughly without further interruptions."

"But I have to come back here eventually."

"I think that if I marry Aillie Rannoch, whom I admired as Anna Rayner, that Glenshael will have enough to digest. It will work, love, you'll see."

"I suppose it will. How funny to be Mrs. Alastair Forres."

"I must remind you that you're still single. What's facing you is your last Rannoch fling. Appropriate for your story up to date. We'll finish off your masquerade with a fine flourish. Kilt up your green kirtle, love, and fly with me. And the de'il tak' the hindmost, bonnie Aillie."

# 18

## Triumph

I HAVE GIVEN an account of how I ran away a second time and went to London.

How very different it was! We were so happy. No homesickness, no insecurity, and far too little hardship. As for loneliness, I forget what it's like. That's why I sometimes try to remember.

At first I made a very douce wife. The trouble was that Alastair just laughed.

"I'm not impressed, Aillie. You're better in romantic parts. Anyhow, I prefer to participate than be an audience."

"I wasn't acting. Ach, you make me wild!"

"Do I? Poor love, you try so hard, and I'm far too happy to care or notice. Relax! Life's wonderful. You're wonderful. I love you as you are, so stay that way."

For a long time I hardly thought about Glenshael. I'd dropped a note to James and the Macdonalds explaining

I had lost my nerve. Nothing else, for Angus and Craigie blurred our trail, and Alastair thought we should lie low till time had smoothed things over. We'd finished our extended honeymoon before we admitted to our marriage. The idea was we should have met abroad. Mrs. McNichol duly read Craigie's postcards and held that it was so—so who would contradict her?

It was soon after our return to London that I ran into Catherine in another cocktail bar.

"What a place to find a heather hunter," I said brightly.

"I don't think I know you," she replied with puzzled doubt.

Then Robin arrived with some drinks.

"Good evening, Anacher," I said.

"Good God! It's Aillie—Aillie Rannoch!"

"Not any more. She was staked at the last crossroads. Do I have to introduce you to the man who did it?"

They stared. No wonder. I was dressed up to kill. We were going to the opera afterwards. And Alastair had altered too. He'd lost his lean and hungry look, was very tanned, and generally laughing. You'd never think he'd been a sourpuss, ever.

"Robin, they're blooming. Have you two got married?"

"Indissolubly," said Alastair, and bought more drinks.

"You always did manage to land on two feet, Aillie, however hard you were pushed," Robin remarked prosaically as we began to celebrate. "But while I am no longer in your income group, I do think, as your only surviving relative of any consequence, you might have asked me to your wedding. I could have given you away,

a gesture to prove I finally shook off immense and unde-
sired responsibility."

"I'm afraid he has no tact," Catherine said. "Though
he really was worried when you disappeared again. But
tell me, how and when did all this happen?"

Alastair and I exchanged glances. Sometimes we found
it difficult to recall the mood which sent us on our wild
elopement.

"Not that we had a grand affair ourselves," she continued, amused enough to save us from reply. "Thank
heavens there is Deborah to redeem our standards. Her
trustees have now agreed to David and St. Margaret's in
the spring. I'm going to have a model hat, whatever
Robin says—and I don't think he should wear the kilt, do
you?"

"I read about Deborah in the glossy papers. She has
become my mascot."

"Mine too. I cut out all the extracts and stick them in a
book, to help pass the time at Ilsafeccan. But she writes
too, quite often, most affectionately. I'm glad to say she's
sounding far more sensible and settled."

The guardians of Deborah's millions named the following April, and, a strange thing, Alastair and I were asked
to the wedding. We wondered if someone had worked
down the funeral list to collect family friends. If so, I
hope she didn't realize.

We all went together, the Macdonalds, Alastair, and I,
and we made a very fine quartet, I think. As for my wee
romantic heroine, she was most beautiful, all virgin-white
and still with parted lips and starry eyes. She drifted by
and smelt of lilies of the valley. I couldn't find my
handkerchief, of course. Alastair lent me his, I cried so

copiously. I didn't like to think how she must stop adventuring and turn into an ordinary girl. That's how it always looks, though if you come to think of it romance does flourish fairly well even when clothed in quiet domestic propriety. I looked at Alastair. No outsider could guess what he was really like. David? Who could say? People have different tastes. Just the same, I hoped and prayed I had done right. That she'd enjoy her bairns and embassies as the mad wife had prophesied. Things had turned out so happily for me, I was apt to think I had a magic touch.

It felt so when we returned to Castle Rannoch. The hills were purple and the ripening trees were golden in the glen. All this and Alastair; my own folk too. They were all so pleased to see me back.

It has become a happy, friendly house. I doubt if it reminds James now of Mrs. Radcliffe. He and Alastair behave like bickering brothers. I won't have any nonsense. I am fond of James.

Alastair finds me overneighbourly. But then he's not gregarious at all. He's too fond of my exclusive company. I sometimes wonder why he likes it so. Poor Alastair! He is improving, and incidentally so am I.

We've had only one real disagreement since we married, but it made up for every one we'd missed. We raged and battled in a major war, and then we didn't even speak for days and days. I'd never go through that again —never. Mind you, I won. I had to.

Mrs. McNichol started it—imagine! Just a quiet scrutiny of my waistline, of which she obviously disapproved. Then it was Angus who took over, far more vocally, enquiring in a most obstetric way.

"Ach, hold your tongue." I nearly shouted. "I've not been married a year yet. Civilized people need a bit of time to settle in together, without a lot of bairns in the way."

To hear me speak, you'd think I had talked it over like a family planner. It wasn't true. I daren't discuss such things with Alastair.

"Himself is looking fine, that I will say. When I heard that you would wed him, I was wondering. You don't know how these illnesses affect the men. I would not say that he was strong forbye."

"You've a mind like a stockman, I am thinking."

"Ach, maybe, but for a' that you are not so young, the two of you, and it's a daft thing for sure to lose good time."

"You talk as if I were yon Sarah in the Bible!"

"Aye, and no angel will be visiting you, young Aillie, so don't be hoping it. You get the bairn and I will sing the psalms."

The same evening when my feathers were still ruffled, Alastair took the idea I should go back to the stage. Perhaps he caught some feeling of frustration, and for the first time misinterpreted my mood.

"I shall not! It's bad enough when both partners are on the stage, when they understand the code. Considering you get jealous of poor James when all he does is call me 'my dear Alice,' I can't see you enjoying me embraced by total strangers. Just as an outlet for my energies! Besides, there's plenty here to keep me occupied, and one day I hope there will be more. This house needs a family, Alastair. And incidentally so do we."

All very bold. The effect was horrifying. He went chalk-white. I couldn't bear to see such fear and pain. Yet this was required of me, so I went on. And on and on, until he cracked. The longer the wrong sort of cowardice stays with a man, the more distorting its effect. We had to bring this in the open. I never liked a job less.

Yet all the time I knew it was quite necessary—for him, for me, and all the content of our future.

The storm blew over, clearing the air between us. He doesn't talk about his first wife often, but when he does he mentions her with pleasure. The tragedy's receded and grown dim, and I often think she's joined my friendly ghosts, never resenting that I give him all he needs. He always said she was a fine person.

In the end I turned into a heroine too. I state the fact with pride. For nine months I was daily buried with my unborn child. Alastair said goodbye each time he looked at me, while all the village talked about my mother and wondered if I'd go the same way to the grave. When the time came—and to my delight and Alastair's dismay, the great event took place at Castle Rannoch—I summoned James as midwife to my husband, then Robin for a specialist opinion. I think they must have held him down by force and doctored him with Dousie alcohol. At any rate, by the morning I felt better than he looked. He takes things so damned hard, Alastair.

No story ends, it just starts again. A new pattern, different runners for the relay. I fancy our wee Flora later on will be slipping down to Holly Bank to broaden her horizons and acquire substantial culture. Like me, she's very fond of James. She grows a little bored with home. Alastair spoils her, Angus and Craigie are too much in her thrall, but James has to be wooed—though mind, he's easily won. I am so ousted these days that I think I'll abdicate, and turn into a douce wife after all.

Postcript. Today, on the front page of the paper, is the story of how the daughter of a foreign banker has eloped to marry her true love in Scotland. Columns and columns, since the news is thin, and a fine photograph of the romantic pair. She is demure; he wears full highland dress; and every time I look at it, I smile. Like Catherine, I plan to cut it out and paste it in the family album.

We ought to have one picture of my interesting cousin, Peter Rannoch.

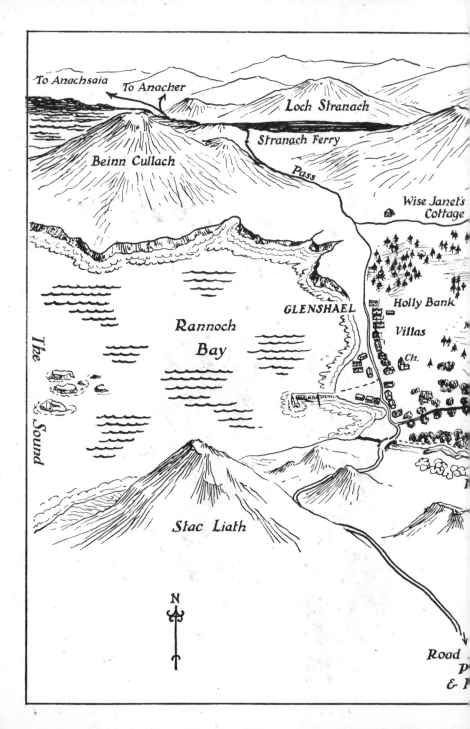

To Anachsaia
To Anacher
Loch Stranach
Stranach Ferry
Pass
Beinn Cullach
Wise Janet's Cottage
GLENSHAEL
Holly Bank
Villas
Ch.
Rannoch Bay
The Sound
Stac Liath
N
Road
P
&